Basted Butchery

ACF Bookens

VINCI
BOOKS

By ACF Bookens

Stitches In Crime

Vinci Books

vinci-books.com

Published by Vinci Books Ltd in 2025

1

A CIP catalogue record for this book is available from the British Library.
Paperback ISBN: 9781036710361

The EU GPSR authorised representative is Logos Europe, 9 rue Nicolas Poussion, 17000 La Rochelle, France
contact@logoseurope.eu

Chapter One

I don't really know what I was thinking when I picked up this cross-stitch kit. I'd been nannying for a friend in Baltimore, and I realized, as I always do when I think I'm going to be all "see the town" in a new place, that all I wanted to do was relax, sew, and watch their limitless supply of TV channels. Their child had been a delight all day, but I was tired. I need something soothing to do, so I ran out to the nearest craft store and bought the funnest kit I could find, thinking I'd make it for my mom.

And that is how, more than a decade later, I was now untangling strands of embroidery floss, trying to figure out how to read the pattern, and deciding if I really wanted to go back in to stitch Maggie, the cat who had made herself at home in the pattern's sewing room. Santiago had taken Sawyer fishing for a week up in West Virginia, and I had a massive salvage job starting on Monday at the farm next door. So this weekend, I was going to sit, stitch, and catch up on all the shows that I couldn't watch while Sawyer was in the house. He thought he was old enough to swear like a sailor, but I still held that age 6 was a bit young for such language. Whew!

After spending the first episode of *High Potential* detangling, I decided I was going to finish the kit. For anyone who knew me, this decision would have come as no surprise because I was a finisher, to a fault. If I hated a meal I'd ordered, rather than ask for something else, I just ate it. A book bored me to tears through three chapters, it didn't matter; I was finishing that sucker. And thus, I had an entire antique hatbox full of half-done projects like this one. I'd just turned 50, and it was time for me to wrap up some stuff or send it on. Since the very idea of sending it on made my heart race, finishing up it was.

In reality, the project didn't matter that much to me as long as I had something to stitch on this quiet, solitary weekend. Sometimes, just the idea of stitching relaxed me, the colors, the patterns, the simplicity of the stitch itself…I could think about it and calm down almost instantly.

This afternoon, though, I was especially excited to get to it because it was still daylight, which meant the stitching was easier on my eyes and because I had hours before my late bedtime of 10pm. There was only so much I was willing to screw up my sleep schedule even when I was going to have a week alone. That 6:30am wake-up on Sawyer's first day back at school was going to be hard enough as it was.

For three hours, I lost myself in ridiculous police drama and stitches, and when I finally gave in to my hunger around 6, I found I was absolutely famished and really had to pee. I had realized that I often did this to myself when I was alone – I just put off my body's needs until they were urgent, not so much out of self-neglect as out of lack of awareness. It had been that way my whole life, in fact. In school, I'd wait to go to the bathroom until I was at home, and it was a close call sometimes, because I was too over-whelmed by everything there to even think about going to the bathroom.

Now, I realized that was part of my ADHD, a diagnosis I'd only gotten in the last year, and while the diagnosis helped me understand why I did that, I hadn't yet landed on the thing that would help me overcome this tendency. I was just counting it a win that I had set a timer on my phone to remind me to drink something every two hours. Clearly, that was why I now had to pee.

I was just coming out of the bathroom with a plan to make myself grilled cheese and tomato soup for dinner when I saw a light across the stream. The farm across the way had been empty for as long as I'd lived here, and while it had been recently sold to a family who wanted to restore it – the family for whom I'd be working next week in fact – it seemed odd that someone would be poking around with what looked like a flashlight at dusk on a Friday evening.

Normally, I would have just let Santi know, but since he was in another state, I decided to just take a ride over there and check it out myself. Of course, I let my best friend Mika know what I was doing, but when I heard her reply come almost immediately, I ignored it. She wasn't going to like that I was going. I, however, was giving myself credit for being responsible enough to tell someone. I hadn't always done that. *Take your win where you can get it, Miks,* I thought.

While the distance to the Brown Plantation over the stream was quite short as the crow flies, the actual road wound around through what used to be a town, over a one-lane bridge, and then up a roadside to a long, gravel drive-way. Walking, I could have been there in 5 minutes. Driving, it took me 7.

When I pulled up to the brick Federal-style house, I felt

a little thrill. The building hadn't been altered much in the last two hundred years since it had been built, and because the enslaved people who built it were clearly skilled crafts-men, the structure was still quite solid and beautiful. I knew the inside had seen better days – the new owners had emailed me some pictures – but the main house and the outbuildings were still very solid.

Not seeing any lights around the big house, I wandered around to the north side, where most of the outbuildings stood. The dairy was still there as were the stables, a black-smith's shed, and the building I was most excited about – the old weavers' shed In the days when the plantation had been built, the women who wove the clothing for everyone on the farm had worked in here, and from the pictures, I knew that two huge spinning wheels were still intact inside. But as excited as I was, I wasn't dumb enough to go poking around in dead buildings alone at dusk. While it wasn't likely we'd have snakes this time of year, we did have black widows and worn-out floorboards. I wasn't keen to spend the night with my leg dangling through a hole while a red-bellied spider decided if I was a threat.

So I just wandered slowly around the buildings. My eyes were pretty accustomed to the dark in the country, some-thing that amazed all my friends who lived in cities, so I didn't turn on the flashlight on my phone. The gloaming gave me plenty of light to see, and my circuit around the buildings didn't reveal anyone. I had just decided maybe it was someone talking a stroll or looking for a lost dog when I caught a flash of light from the corner of my eye. It was heading into the woods behind the outbuildings, up and away from the stream.

I was reckless, but I wasn't that reckless. So I just waited to be sure they didn't come back, and then I started back toward my car, looking up the new owner's number as I went. I stood by my car, debating whether or not to tell them what had just happened. I decided against it, though, since it didn't seem like anything had been disturbed. No need to worry them unnecessarily. Then, just as I was opening my car door, I heard the sound of a loud truck engine off in the direction that the light had gone.

It used to be that I knew nothing about trucks, but since I'd married a man whose one country streak related to pick-ups, I'd learned a lot. I could tell from the sound of the engine that the muffler had been straightened to make it louder, and when it turned onto the paved road, I heard the wheeze of the mud tires. That wasn't enough to differentiate it from all the other loud pick-ups with mud tires, but it was something.

For now, though, I needed food, a glass of wine, and more TV and sewing. As soon as I turned down my driveway, though, I saw Mika's little sedan in the driveway, and then, I noticed that she was sitting on my porch, a quilt wrapped around her, and her phone in her hand. As soon as I opened the car door, she said, "I was giving it two more minutes, and then I was calling the police."

I rolled my eyes. "I'm fine. No problems," I said. "I just didn't want to take any risks by going out without letting someone know where I was." I started to walk past her and invite her into the house where I had, of all things, heat, but her open-mouthed stared caught my attention even in the periphery. "What?"

"You seriously think that going to an abandoned farm after dark alone isn't risky?" She stared at me harder.

"Well, no, but at least I texted you, right?"

"Right. So I could worry without the ability to do

anything about it except to do what might have been considered overreacting. That's a great choice."

She was really mad, and while I didn't fully understand why, I definitely hadn't intended to worry her. I turned and put my hands on her arms. "I'm sorry, Miks. I didn't mean to worry you." I held her gaze until she let out a long sigh, and I knew that she was okay. "I'm really sorry."

She wrapped her arm around my waist. "Thank you for apologizing. Can we go in now? I need to sit by your fire."

"Of course," I said. "Did you bring a project? Because I have soup, grilled cheese, and some more TV to watch."

She pointed to a tote bag next to my kitchen peninsula. "Of course, and tomato soup?"

"You know it," I said. The two of us fell into an easy rhythm, making my comfort dinner just the way my mom had made it – sliced grocery store, whole wheat bread, thick slices of sharp cheddar, lots of butter, and tomato soup made with the requested one can of water. No special herbs. No cream. No fancy spread on the bread. Just basic as the days when she made it for me after snowball fights. Mika knew the drill, and soon, we were settled back in with our food on the ottoman, our handwork at our side, and our eyes glued to the television.

Normally, I might have resented someone interrupting my weekend of solitude, but having Mika with me was like being with myself but funnier. I had someone to snark with, and she alternated trips to the kitchen with me when we needed more wine or snacks. But she didn't require me to be anyone but myself. This is why she was my best friend.

We stayed up way too late one-more-episode-ing ourselves, but eventually, she climbed into Sawyer's bed and I into mine, and when I finally dragged myself from bed the next morning, she was gone, a note on the table that said,

"Don't sew too hard." It was a sort of private joke with us because we'd both given ourselves repetitive use injuries from our sewing and crocheting. She was teasing, but she also wasn't. Neither of us wanted to have hand surgery.

So rather than just immediately sitting back down, turning on my audio book, and starting to stitch again, I puttered about the house a bit, doing the kind of things I usually just ignored because I didn't have the time, focus, or energy. So by the time I returned to my slightly concave cushion on the couch, the cabinet doors were gleaming, Beauregard's litter box was deep-cleaned, and the laundry was actually already in the dryer.

If Beau, the Maine Coon, had been a dog, I would have considered that his desire to snuggle up close and go to sleep as soon as I sat down was gratitude for his clean bathroom, but I knew better. He was cold. I was warm-blooded. He would tolerate me so that he could siphon away my heat, just as he tolerated the walk to the car in the winter because he could take full advantage of the heated seat as I chauffeured him around his fiefdom.

Still, I welcomed the quiet rumble of his begrudging purr and did, indeed, stitch the day away. But as dusk began to settle, I found myself at the front windows of my house watching the Brown Plantation to see if I saw lights there again. I didn't, and most of me was relieved ...except for that little part that was just so curious about what someone had been doing over there the night before.

Fortunately, I saw that a new episode of *Rescue: High Surf* had become available on streaming, and I was distracted enough by that prospect to put away the twinge of a thought that might have sent me back there to poke around again. These kinds of urges never hit me in daylight, when my brain was fully functional and the tiredness of a day of

7

doing almost nothing hadn't zapped me. And I reminded myself that if I went, tomorrow not only would Mika and Santi be mortified, I would probably feel a bit chagrined myself.

Instead, I forced myself to watch beautiful people in a beautiful place saving lives and creating drama in their own. Then, I picked up the grumpy cat and went to bed.

Sunday rolled by in much the same way as Saturday, except perhaps less productively. Aside from the enjoyment and nostalgia I got attending services with my friend Mary from time to time, I wasn't much of a church goer anymore. As I told most people, God and I were good, but the church and I had some stuff to work out. Still, though, that Sabbath day was built into my life's rhythm, so I was able to let myself fully relax on Sundays without guilt even. So I took full advantage and just lazed and napped and stitched all day, living off granola bars and my water bottle. It was simple but luxurious.

Plus, the effects of all that rest and relaxation were that when Monday morning rolled around, I was genuinely energized and excited to get to work over at the Brown Place, and not just because I was curious to see if I could figure out why someone had been poking around in the dark. I was scheduled to meet the new owners over there at 9am, so about 8:30, when I had resisted the urge to go over for a full hour and had chosen to fold my laundry instead, I got my new high-resolution camera (a Christmas present from my husband), my notebook, and my pen and headed over, walking this time.

When I made it up the hill by the big house just before 9, I was slightly sweaty but even more energetic, my blood really pumping from the steep hike up the hill from the stream. Fortunately, though, I was the first one there, so I had a few minutes to catch my breath. Nothing like huffing and puffing through your first in-person meeting with your new clients.

While I let my heart rate settle, I strolled around the property, this time peeking in windows and open outbuilding doors rather than both hoping and not hoping that I would find someone else there. Instead, I was mentally cataloging possible items to salvage – windows and floorboards, mostly, but I also saw a great mantel in one room, and I wasn't sure, but I thought there might have still been an anvil in the blacksmith's shop.

The new owners, the Abramses, were a couple from DC. The plantation was going to be their vacation home but also a place where they focused the storytelling around the people who had been enslaved there. The aim was to have a high-end hotel that was available at a more moderate price than many of the fine hotels in the area and that was intended to draw African American visitors. Thus, they were renovating all the outbuildings to be guest suites, but they were also going to keep them thematically connected to their original purposes.

So unlike the buildings that I usually salvaged from, where things were going to be gutted or demolished, the Abramses wanted to save as much as they could while also being reasonable about what was needed to make the space a luxury hotel. That's why we were meeting today – they wanted to inventory what I would take and what, in my opinion, could be saved and used with a little polish. So we were planning a day of inspecting everything to help with my salvage plans and their remodeling ones.

I was just walking up onto the front porch of the main house when I heard tires crunching behind me. There, in their beautiful maroon Cadillac, were Willie and William

Abrams. They had immediately joked about their names when we first talked, and their ability to see the humor in themselves had won me over immediately. Willie was a small woman with long braids, skinny jeans, and the best bejeweled eyeglasses I'd ever seen. William was tall and broad-shouldered, built like a lineman, which made sense since he had played professional football in his not-so-distant past. I waved enthusiastically as they walked toward the house, and when Willie stepped up next to me and gave me a hug, I immediately liked her, and not just because she smelled like coconut and fresh air. She actually hugged me, tight. I loved a person who gave me a real hug.

William stooped slightly and put out his oven mitt of a hand for me to shake. My fingers barely encircled his, but his smile took away any intimidation I might have felt at his size. "Paisley, it's so nice to meet you," he said in a resonant voice. "Thank you for meeting us here. I hope you didn't have to come far."

I laughed and pointed behind me. "I can see your new place from mine. I'm in the little blue house across the bridge."

"What?!" Willie said. "We're going to be neighbors. See, another sign that we are on the right path." She looked at her husband and winked.

"Never doubted it," he said. "So where do we start, Ms. Salvage?"

I chuckled and thought, for a second, about what that name might look like on a T-shirt. But I forced myself to focus and said, "If it's okay with you, let's start in the main house. Since you'll be living there, I imagine you're going to want to get it livable first."

"Actually," Willie said, "We're going to live in the old weavers' shed, leave the big house for guests."

"Oh," I said, my affection for these people growing by the minute. "I love that. Do you want to start there, instead?"

"Yes, let's," William said. "We're not going to do anything fancy in there. Just a comfortable bedroom and bath."

"You know, I think that's so wise. I really value my alone time, and this way you guys will have yours," I said as we walked to the shed.

"That's exactly what we were thinking. We'll mingle with our guests at meals and in the kitchen, but it'll also be nice to have our own place to relax and get a break," Willie said as she pushed open the unlatched door on the shed. "That's odd," she said as she flipped the open padlock on the door. "I thought we'd locked this up."

"We were in and out so fast last time …we probably just forgot," William said.

Once again, I debated on whether or not to say anything about the visitor from Friday. I decided, though, that it was best to be forthright, so I quickly mentioned that I'd seen a light up here, that I'd come to check it out, and that I'd seen the person leave without, as far as I could tell, disturbing anything.

William frowned at me. "You came up here by yourself?"

"He was here by the shed when I arrived." I didn't say anymore, but my implication was clear.

William bent down to look at the dangling lock. "It doesn't look like it's been broken or jimmied." He dropped the lock. "We're the only ones with a key, so we must have just forgotten." He looked at his wife and smiled. "It's okay."

She didn't look convinced, and I certainly had a lot of

questions that led me to my own doubts. Had they put the lock on the door, or had it already been there? Could anyone else – like the realtor or a handyman – have a copy of the key? Was this one of those locks that could be picked with a ballpoint pen? I didn't say anything, though. Everything did look fine, and withal the trouble of the world, why borrow more?

The door opened smoothly, and inside, I was delighted to see that the floors were in good shape. "These can just be cleaned and kept, in my opinion." The boards were wide and rough and old. Heart pine, it looked like. "If you don't mind a little more rough texture."

"They are gorgeous," Willie said, bending down and running her fingers over the boards. "Yes, we'll keep those."

"The windows are in great shape, and they have original glass. But they'll not be terribly efficient or warm. That's your call," I continued as I moved around the roughly fifteen foot by fifteen foot space.

The couple looked to one another, and I took a few steps away to give them the privacy I could in the small room. The back wall featured a fireplace made from hand-shaped bricks, and a small beam served as a rough mantel.

"If you'll take the windows, Paisley," Willie said, "we'll replace them with more efficient ones."

I made a note and then pointed at the fireplace. "You'll want to have this evaluated if you want to use it. I expect that at the least you'll need to have it repointed, but it might also need a sleeve."

"We won't use it," William said. "Can you salvage the bricks and the mantel?"

"I can," I said, secretly delighted and peered behind the bricks. "It looks like the wall is in pretty good shape behind it, but of course there will be some repair work that needs to be done."

"We've already contracted with Saul to do the repair work," William said. "Based on your fine recommendation."

Saul was Mika's biological uncle and my adopted one. He was an expert historical contractor and also the landlord for my architectural salvage shop that sat on his construction lot. He was one of my favorite people in the world, and I was glad to hear the Abramses had hired him.

"Excellent," I said. "He'll know just what to do here." I made another note and then, finally, addressed the items that had caught my eye as soon as we walked in – long bolts of vintage fabrics all stacked in the corner of the room and two spinning wheels. "How about this fabric?" I said.

"It's beautiful," Willie said as she fingered what looked to be a paisley pattern on a dupioni silk. "But we don't have any need of it, right?" She looked to her husband.

"Nope," he agreed.

"Not even for curtains or such?" I could feel my excitement building, but before I got my hopes up about the delight these bolts of fabric would elicit in my customer base, I wanted to be sure the Abramses were sure.

"Nope, we're going with a more modern palette," Willie said and then laughed. "I sound so pretentious."

"Next time I come over, I'll expect you to be wearing white gloves and smoking a cigarette in a holder," I joked.

"Better that than some plantation hoop skirt or some such," William said with a chuckle.

"Very true," I said. "Okay, I'll take these with me today, probably. Just to clear the space for the rest of the retrieval." I looked up at the ceiling, which was exposed beams and the roof boards under the metal sheeting above. "If I were you, I'd just clean that up and leave it. It's beautiful." I smiled at my new clients. "But of course, if you need me to help with anything else in here, let me know."

"And you'll take the spinning wheels, of course," Willie said.

I grinned. "I'd love to, again, if you don't want them for décor," I said.

"We're not using anything more about the enslaved people's labor than is necessary for the running of the hotel. We're reclaiming this space as our own," William said. "So no, as beautiful and important as they are, we will not be using them."

"Understood," I said and made a mental note to consider how I might repurpose one of these to reclaim it the same way.

We moved on to the wagon shed, which included several wagon wheels and an old Coca-Cola chest cooler. William claimed the cooler for the bar space he was creating in the basement of the house, but the wheels were all mine. Most of the other outbuildings were full of old furniture, all of which I offered to take and dispose of if it wasn't salvageable. The Abramses agreed, and we entered the main house to do our final round of scouting. Here, the couple wanted to keep most of the finer elements – the mantels, the wainscotting, the chair rails and crown moulding. They didn't say as much, but I gathered they wanted to have these adornments for the same reason they didn't want to have the reminders of labor – the people who had created them, the talented craftspeople that they were, were not allowed to enjoy the fruits of their own fine labor. Now, though, maybe some of their descendants would, and if not their direct kin, at least those people who inherited freedom from their perseverance and determination.

I did make note of the windows in the house since they

were going to be replaced with exact replicas that were much more efficient. And there was a classic set of sunshine yellow kitchen appliances that, as best I could tell, were all in working order that the Abramses were delighted to hear I'd rid them of.

My plan was to come back with Saul and his crew the next day to load a truck with most of the items, but today, I wanted to get a look at that fabric and put it up on my site. My Subaru was just big enough to fit all the rolls, so I headed back to the weavers' House with William to get them out of the building. It took us a couple of trips, but we managed to get the first eight rolls into the station wagon without any trouble. I was headed back from the car to get some of the final few rolls when I heard William shout for help.

I sprinted the rest of the way to the shed, but I came to a fast stop when I saw that William was holding a roll of plastic with a human head sticking out.

"Call the police," he said.

Chapter Two

Of course, my first instinct was to text Santi. He was always faster to respond than 911, even though both his officers and the EMTs were excellent, but I had given my son my word that I wouldn't interrupt their week. Sawyer was very excited to spend the week with his stepdad, and I knew that if he got wind of this situation, he would be home within hours. I wouldn't do that to Sawyer, not when Santi's staff was quite capable of handling the situation.

So like any normal Octonia citizen, I called 911, told the dispatcher that we'd found a body at the old Brown place, and asked her to send officers and am ambulance. I couldn't imagine that anyone who had been wrapped in plastic was still alive, but I also wasn't willing to take a chance on that.

Then, I slipped my phone into my pocket and helped William lay the body down flat on the floor of the shed. The person was slight, but a human body was heavy, especially when said human couldn't help move their own body.

"Now, we need to leave him be," I said to William. He

had started to unwrap the plastic but stopped immediately. "The police will need to see him as he is."

William took a few steps back. "Right. Right," he said. "So you think he's a man, too."

"I do," I said, "but of course, he'll need to be identified for us to be sure of his gender."

"Right, right," William said again. "Of course."

I didn't think my client was actually processing much of anything at the moment, and I couldn't blame him. Unfortunately, I'd found more than my fair share of dead bodies, and while I would definitely have to take some time and process this experience later, I was past the initial shock. "Why don't we go sit on the porch? Let Willie know what happened."

I put my hand on the small of the giant man's back and steered him to the porch, where I pointed at the rocking chair and told him to sit. Then, I went in and found Willie, where she was unpacking dishes into the kitchen cabinets. "Can you come to the porch?" I said.

She put down the stack of simple, white plates and followed me out the door. "What's wrong?" she asked as she saw her husband sitting with his head in his hands.

I quickly told her that we had found a body in the weavers' shed and that the police were on the way. "I didn't know him," I said and only then realized what a strange thing that was to say. Of course I didn't know him.

Willie nodded at me. "Okay, Okay." She put her hand on William's back and began making small circles, like the ones my mom used to make on my back to comfort me, like the ones I made on Sawyer's now. Just the sight of the gestured calmed me a bit.

Moments later, I heard tires on the gravel drive and went out to meet Alan Forest, my husband's deputy. The man had become a good friend to us in the few months since he'd started working at the Octonia Sheriff's Office, and he was a good police officer. So while he smiled at me when I greeted him, he was all business and went immediately to the Abramses. "Ma'am, sir," he said. "I'm Deputy Forest. Can you tell me what you found?"

William looked up at me, and I gave him a nod. I was there, too, but this was his property. It was better he take the lead on the situation rather than deferring to me, even if I was the sheriff's wife. "There's a body," he said. "Over there." He pointed toward the weavers' shed. "It's wrapped in plastic. Was hidden behind some bolts of fabric."

"Some of those bolts are in my car because they were salvaged, but I'll get them back out if need be," I added.

"Did you recognize him?" Forest said after a curt nod to acknowledge my statement.

William shook his head and so did I. "Never seen him before," I said and noted Forest's quick note.

"Anything else you noticed that I should know about?" the deputy asked.

Willie and William looked at me, and I took a deep breath. "Yes, on Friday night, I saw someone snooping around the property."

Forest's eyebrows furrowed. "I need the details please. Were you here?"

I nodded and then quickly recounted what I had seen both from home and from up here at the Abrams's place. I even went so far as to describe the sound of the truck and its tires. "You know those mud tires, the ones that sound like a rocket launching when they get going?" I finished.

A small smile played at the corner of Forest's mouth. "Yes, I know what mud tires sound like, Paisley." He glanced up from his notebook. "I'm actually kind of impressed you do, though."

I sighed. "Grow up in the country and date enough country boys, you begin to innately know all kinds of things that you wished you could use that brain space for."

"Well, in this case, your ear for tire sounds might just come in handy." He looked at each of us as he said, "Anything else?"

We all shook our heads, and he slipped the notebook and pen back into his pocket. "Alright then. I need to look around. If you'll just point me to the body. . ."

William led him over to the weavers' shed and then waited outside while the deputy examined the body. "I'll need to call the coroner and get crime scene techs out here, but it looks like he was strangled …and some time ago."

As the deputy took his phone out of his pocket, I asked, "What do you mean 'some time ago?'"

"Can't be sure until we get word from the coroner, but I think our victim was embalmed."

The shiver that ran through my body made my teeth clack together.

"What do you mean he was embalmed? Like a mummy?" Willie's eyes were wide, and there was a quaver in her voice.

"Like I said, I'm not sure, but I thought I smelled formaldehyde." He looked at me and gave a subtle shake of his head.

"Let's not think about that," I said. "Willie, do you have some tea in there? Maybe with a shot of whiskey?"

My question seemed to jerk her thoughts away from the body, and she, as most Southern woman are inclined to do by training if not by choice, turned into a hostess on the spot. "Yes, I do. Deputy, may I bring you some tea?"

"Yes, ma'am," Forest said with an actual tip of his ball cap. "No whiskey for me, though, being as I'm on duty and all."

She gave him a small smile, and when William looked at me, I tilted my head as a suggestion that he follow.

"Now, what are you saying, Deputy?" I whispered as soon as the couple was out of ear shot.

He leaned toward me. "You've seen enough dead bodies to know what they look like just after death, right?"

I shuddered but nodded my head. Unfortunately, I did know.

"Well, this one doesn't look, er, fresh," he said with a wince. "Maybe I'm wrong. Tell me if I am."

I followed him back to the weavers' shed, and for the first time, I looked down at the victim. Forest wasn't wrong. This man had been dead for a while, but he didn't look like he was decaying. Maybe *mummifying* was the better word. "I see what you mean," I said and stepped back out of the shed. I didn't need even more images of dead people clouding my mind on the daily, but it was curious, disturbing, too, that this person had been dead for a while and was just in the shed.

A thought occurred to me. "Do you think whoever was here on Friday night might have put the body there then? Or do you think it's been here since, well, since it was prepared?"

Forest shook his head. "I don't know, Pais. But it's definitely odd. I could hazard a lot of theories right now, but I'm going with Santi's way on this one."

"Follow the evidence," I said in a slightly deeper voice that I lilted to mimic the slight hint of a Mexican accent that he had inherited from his mother.

Forest smiled. "Exactly."

For the next while, Willie, William, and I sat on the front porch with our tea and some shortbread that Willie had brought along from DC and watched the coroner and the crime scene team do their work. The body was loaded into the coroner's van just a few short minutes after she arrived. I missed my old friend who had served in the coroner's office and left for maternity leave a couple months ago, and I had yet to meet the new one. But it didn't seem like a casual introduction was appropriate as she wheeled a mummified body away.

The crime scene techs took a bit longer, and while I still wasn't entirely sure what those specialists actually did, the three of us had a good time imagining which of the young people was Warrick, which Gil, and which Nick. Since they were all men, we didn't have the pleasure of deciding who was Catherine, but we did get a good chuckle out of making up hokey, sciencey dialogue for the team. Probably not the most respectful way of handling the situation, but it helped us stay calm while we waited for them to complete their work.

When they were done, Forest told us that we needed to leave the shed closed for the time being to preserve the scene unless they needed to come back, and he advised the Abrams's that they might want to lock the gate at the end of the drive for a while, even when they were here, just to keep the overly curious from driving up and claiming they were lost.

After Forest assured me, again, that he wouldn't call Santi unless absolutely necessary, he headed back to the station to begin the formal investigation. As his car headed down the drive, William looked at me and said, "He's just being over cautious about the gate, right?"

"Nope," I said. "I once had a yard sale at my place, and two hundred people showed up and boldly declared that they had just "always wanted to see my house up close." I'd lock the gate."

Willie nodded. "Do we even have a lock?"

"Hang tight," I said and went to the back of my Subaru. I wasn't always the most prepared person, but I did carry a lot of stuff in my car, mostly because I was married to the sheriff and the mother of a young, busy, mechanically minded son. So after carefully moving aside the bolts of fabric that Forest had said I could keep if I still wanted them, shifting over the jumper cables, space blanket, hand-warmers, flare gun, and full tool set that Santi asked me to carry, and shoving all the sports equipment that Sawyer now left in the car on the regular, I found what I was looking for – a long length of silver chain and a padlock that I had salvaged from a job sometime back and had thought I might use to secure a future job site if needed. "Here you go," I said, the chain and lock hanging from my hand as I walked back to the porch.

"You just happened to have that in your Subaru?" William said with a wry smile.

"Yes, sir. My car is not only the brand of choice for American lesbians, but it's also the choice of single moms who do messy work, are prone to get stuck in snow and mud, and who carry a lot of junk around all the time." Kristin Key was one of my favorite comedians, and I had been preparing that line about single moms to heckle her with if I ever saw her in person and Subarus came up. Since they came up in almost every show of hers that I'd watched,

I thought I was probably going to be able to use it someday. I just hadn't thought it would be in relation to a murder.

Willie took the chain and said, "Thank you." Then she sighed. "So what now? Do you want to keep working? Or is this all a bit too much?"

I smiled softly but refrained from saying that if every time I found a dead body I quit that job, Sawyer and I would be homeless and Subaru-less. "Let's call it for today. It's been a long one already. But I'll be back tomorrow. I'll start on the other outbuildings." I looked from her to her husband. "If that's okay with you."

They both nodded. "Yes, that's great. We don't want to be disrespectful," William said, "but we are eager to get the hotel open. Your work is the first step."

"I totally understand. I'll be back in the morning. And I'll bring muffins." My stepmother was a stellar baker, and when I told her and my dad about this situation, I knew she'd want to bake something for the Nicolas's. Plus, I hoped she and Dad might come help me out tomorrow. Normally, I didn't mind working alone, but I didn't relish the thought of going through another long-unused building by myself.

———————

Fortunately, both my dad and stepmom were free the next day, Dad's woodworking class at the senior center being cancelled for the week, so they showed up at my house at 8:30 with muffins, coffee, and what looked distinctly like the shot gun my dad had tried hunting with once when I was in high school.

"You brought a weapon?" I said as my eyebrows lifted to

23

meet my hairline. "Do you even remember how to shoot that thing?"

"He was practicing last night in the yard," my stepmother Lucille said. "Until the police came."

"You were shooting a shotgun at night," I shouted. "Dad, even you know that's illegal."

"Deputy Forest reminded me but then he also noted that he appreciated my diligence to safety when using firearms." Dad grinned. "So I took that as permission."

I rolled my eyes. One of the things about living in a small community like Octonia was that everyone knew everyone and almost everyone's business. I was certain that Forest had known exactly what was happening when he responded to the complaint about shooting after dark at my dad's house, and I was equally certain that he had been happy to see my dad preparing to defend his "baby girl" especially since Santi was away. What surprised me was that someone had called the police about anyone shooting out by where Dad and Lucille lived.

But when I said that, Lucille laughed. "Oh, honey, I called. I couldn't get him to stop, so I called for back-up."

"That makes a lot more sense," I said. "Well, I don't think you'll need the gun today, Dad, but thanks for thinking of keeping us safe."

"Better safe than sorry," he said and held out a handful of shotgun shells to show me. "It's not loaded. Yet."

I sighed. "Okay, let's go. Those muffins smell so good, and I'm eager to introduce you to the Abramses."

Willie and William were already hard at work when we came up the drive. The gate, which they'd locked behind me when I left yesterday morning, was open, and the couple was carefully weeding the front beds around the large boxwoods that flanked the front walk. "Good morning," Willie said as we got out of the car.

"Morning," I said. "I hope you don't mind, but I brought some help."

"And we brought breakfast," Lucille added with a grin. "I'm Lucille, Paisley's stepmom, and this is my husband Lee. He brought muscles." She smiled at her husband. And she wasn't wrong. Even at 78, my dad was the strongest man I knew. He was slowing down some, but he had been doing hard labor all his life and wasn't about to stop now.

"Nice to meet you," William said as he stepped forward to shake Dad's hand.

"And you had to brag about *my* muscles, honey," Dad said with a look at William's bicep, which was roughly the size of my thigh. "I'll just be going home now."

"Absolutely not," Willie said with a laugh. "My daddy can take William here out in two seconds flat. Athlete muscle ain't nothing compared to farm muscle," she said as she looped her arm through Dad's. "But let's not embarrass him."

Dad laughed, and William shook his head. "Please come in." He led us all up the steps into the living room, where the Abramses had managed to arrange some camping stools and three ladder-backed chairs that I had told them were probably original to the house and well-worth restoring and using. Lucille set the carafe of coffee and the tray of muffins on the little table in the center of our casual circle, and Willie brought out mugs, half and half and sugar and set them down with napkins. Everyone dug in, and it was a few minutes before we managed to start talking, so good were Lucille's muffins.

"I'm so glad they're gluten-free," Willie said after Lucille had told her that she only baked gluten-free now since her

Celiac diagnosis. "I don't have a formal diagnosis, but gluten and I just aren't friends anymore. You'll have to give me this recipe."

"Absolutely," Lucille said. "And if you don't bake much, I can show you some tricks. Retirement has given me lots of time to experiment."

Willie grinned, and the two women launched into a discussion of all the substitutions and replacements they'd begun using since they were no longer eating gluten. The men and I listened for a few minutes, and then Dad said, "I'm glad someone is finally moving back into this old place. It's a beauty." He looked around and admired the high ceilings and wide crown molding. "They don't build them like this anymore."

"No, they don't," William said with a small smile. "My ancestors knew what they were doing." I could see William's body tense just a bit after he made this statement, and I knew why. Any talk of slavery was risky in a rural community like ours, and if you wanted to talk about your kin to those people, that quadrupled the risk.

But my dad, as much of a country boy as he was, had worked hard to weed out the racism that had been taught to him in every minute of his childhood, and he just said, "Yes, they did. Were your people here at this plantation?" Dad and I had talked often about the importance of language, about how calling something a *farm* erased the history of the enslaved people who had labored there.

William shrugged. "I don't really know," he said. "We have some stories that tie us back here to Octonia, but nothing on paper." He sighed.

"Would you like me to look into that for you? See what I can find?" I asked. "Happy to do it, no charge."

He looked at me. "You'd do that?"

26

"Happy to," I said. "It's sort of become part of the work I do. Getting the stories of the places I salvage from. Nothing I'd like more than to see if we can connect your people to this plantation or another one here, give some more information for your family' s story …that is if you'd like me to do the work."

"I would, indeed. I've tried, and so has my sister. But we just don't have the time or the knowledge to get very far." He smiled at me.

"Would you mind getting me the names of your parents, grandparents, and any great-grandparents beyond that if you know them? And if you have birth and death dates for people that would help, too. That should be enough to get me started."

A smile broke across William's face, the first real one I'd seen since we found the body the day before. "That would be wonderful. Willie," he said, "Sorry to interrupt, but Paisley is going to do some genealogical digging for me."

Willie clapped her hands once. "Hot dog. That's wonderful."

"If you think you have ancestors here, too, I'm happy to do your family tree as well," I said, careful to not imply anything about who she was descended from. It was simply rude and ignorant to assume that everyone black had enslaved ancestry – I'd learned that over the years I'd been doing this work.

"Paisley Sutton, you are a kind woman. My people are from here, actually, the Gohannas. They were enslaved by the Garths, I believe. Mostly down in Albemarle but up this way, too, I think."

My heart started to beat more quickly. "We have a Garth Road just west of here, and the old Garth place is still standing. Maybe your people were there."

Willie nodded. "Could be." She grew quiet, then, and I decided it was best to leave further conversation along this line to another time. I had no idea what it was like to have ancestors who had been enslaved by other human beings, but my friends who did told me that sometimes, the idea of it was almost too much to bear. So I'd learned not to push when people didn't seem to want to share.

"Well, shall we get started?" Dad said, never a man to sit around when he could be working. "Do you need some help with the garden?"

I grinned. My dad would take garden work over inside work any day.

"If Paisley doesn't need you," William glanced at me, "we'll take all the help we can get."

"I don't need you or Lucille actually, not right now. Maybe when I get into the big house here and have more room, but for now, even two of us in some of the sheds and such might be one too many." I had, in fact, been hoping my dad would help me get the windows out of the old kitchen, but I couldn't deprive him of the chance to work in a historic garden. And Lucille and Willie were getting on so well that I didn't want to separate them either.

So while the four of them returned to the beds in front of the house, I made my way around the corner to the kitchen, refusing to even look at the weavers' shed. I couldn't let my mind dwell on what I'd seen there, not when I had work to do.

For the next hour, I poured myself into my work. I began by cleaning everything out of the kitchen – a couple pewter pitchers, a clay crock that looked quite old, and the sort of detritus that people with old houses always accrue. By the time I was done hauling out the various lengths of trim work, the boxes of old doorknobs and kitchen pulls, and the quite impressive collection of various types of insulation, I was a sweaty, grimy mess, and I was smiling.

A lot of these items were things I could sell, and the rest was probably useful to Saul when he came to begin repair work on the house. But it was the old windows that I really wanted. Their wavy glass was beautiful and in high demand for people who wanted to use it for eccentric greenhouses or even as artwork. Fortunately, I was now old hat at removing antique windows, so I was able to remove the trim, loosen the sashes, and remove the two windows without even having to take out the pulleys or weights attached to them. The fact that the windows would, in fact, actually work if cleaned and re-hung properly gave them even more value, and I found myself quite excited.

That is, until Willie called for me a bit frantically. I ran around to the front of the house just in time to see William put his phone in his back pocket. "They've identified the dead man. His name was Dudley Davenport, and he used to own this house."

Chapter Three

"I've never heard that name," Willie said as we sat on the porch and Lucille went to get the sweet tea that Willie had said was in the fridge. "We didn't buy the house from anyone named Davenport."

"No, but remember, we did get it on a bank auction, so we don't really know who lived here beforehand." William scrubbed his chin. "I wonder if we can find out when he lived here."

"Sure can," I said and stepped off the porch to make a quick phone call. Normally, I'd go to the Clerk of the Court's office and look up the old titles myself, but this wasn't a normal situation. I knew that having some more information on Davenport would help the Abramses. Plus, I had to admit I was very curious.

"Hello," a woman said into the line.

"Trista, is that you?" I asked.

"Yes, this is Trista Tretheway. Who may I ask is calling?"

"Trista, it's Paisley Sutton. I need a favor." It was not in my nature to ask for help, but I'd found I was more inclined to do so when the help was for someone else. "Can you do a title search for me? It's kind of important."

"Absolutely," she said, and I could hear her chair roll back from her desk. "Do you know the plat number?"

"Not off-hand, but it's a recent purchase by William and Willie Abrams. Is that enough?"

"One sec," she said. "Got it." She repeated the plat number, which I typed quickly into my phone for future reference, and then said, I'll call you back in ten."

"Thanks, Trista. Drinks at trivia are on me."

"Sounds good." She hung up, and I made my way back up the stairs to the porch. "We'll know more in a few minutes."

William nodded. "But you knew him, Mr. Sutton?"

"*Knew* might be too strong a word, but yes, I knew of Mr. Davenport. He lived here a long time, like twenty or thirty years," Dad said. "But he kind of kept to himself. Every once in a while, someone would say they heard music and laughter coming from the house, but no one I knew was ever there for those parties, if that's what they were."

"When was this, Dad?" I asked.

Dad looked up at the sky. "Well, you had just left for college, so maybe twenty-five years ago or so." He sighed. "Best I can recall, he moved out. Didn't tell anyone where he was going. Just one day, the house was up for auction by the bank, and everyone assumed he'd died. He was up there in years, as I recall."

"Well, it doesn't look like he moved out at all," Lucille said and then looked up at Willie. "Oh, I'm sorry, that was insensitive."

"No," Willie said. "I was thinking the same thing. He's been here all along."

I nodded. "Might be, or – and I'm not sure this is any

better – maybe the person who was here on Friday brought him?"

Willie shivered. "Yeah, that's not better." She sat forward and put her head in her hands. "All we wanted was to do a nice thing for our community."

"And you will," Lucille said as she put her hand on Willie's back. "We'll help in every way we can."

For the next bit, we all sat silently Eventually, though, I figured that it was the Abramses' prerogative to be still and ponder as long as they wanted, but I had a job to finish. I stood up slowly. "I'm going to get back to it," I said. "Dad, can you help me for a bit?"

My dad heaved himself to his feet. "Sure, Paisley." He glanced at Lucille who gave him a quick nod.

"Alright, I'm getting back to this weeding," she said as she stood up, too.

"Might as well get something done," Willie said, and I heard two more chairs slide a bit on the porch.

Good, I thought. I really wanted my new friends to succeed with this business, and while it would have been completely reasonable for them to give up and sell the plantation, I hoped they wouldn't. Continuing to work, even if it was only to pull weeds, was forward momentum, and they were, I expected, going to need all of it they could get.

Dad and I finished removing the last of the trim on the window I'd abandoned when Willie had called, and then he helped me move things to the front of the house, where the Abramses began to look over what I'd pulled out. They decided the pewter pitchers were really all they wanted besides the wood trim that matched what was elsewhere in the house. So Dad and I made a station near the driveway for the things I'd be taking, and I texted Saul to let him

32

know we had a load if he or one of his crew had time to come pick it up.

"I was on my way over anyway. Got the pick-up. Big enough?" Saul texted right back.

I told him that would be plenty for this load and felt relief lower my shoulders because Saul's presence would mean that we all had something else to focus on for the rest of the day.

Just as Saul's white pick-up pulled in the driveway, my phone rang. It was Trista. "Did you find anything?" I said without even a hello.

"I did," she said, equally to the point. "The house has been in the hands of First National for about 12 years. They've been paying the taxes, and apparently, according to what I could find in the newspaper archives, they've tried to sell it twice before without success."

"And the person who owned it before the bank?" My heart was pounding.

"A man named Dudley Davenport. He was there for 27 years, according to the title. And the bank bought the property after he lapsed on his taxes for two years," Trista said.

"Thank you," I told her. "I'll explain over those drinks soon, okay?"

A lot of the work of my high school classmate involved property transfers and tax payments, so she was very discreet by trade. I knew she wasn't going to ask a lot of questions, but I also knew she was smart and would put things together when the local news got word of the murder. In fact, the fact that it hadn't hit the Charlottesville TV stations yet was somewhat of a miracle. Forest must have been very careful who he shared information with because news like this was absolute fuel for the gossip fire in Octonia.

I walked over to where Saul was talking with the Abramses and my parents and listened as William finished filling him in on the events of the past two days. Saul sighed. "That is a true tragedy. I didn't know Dudley well, but he was a good man."

"You knew him?" Willie asked.

"I did. Saw him in town sometimes. Even had dinner with him here once." Saul gestured toward the house. "He and his husband were quite lovely, but . . ." He trailed off.

"But not everyone in Octonia thought so," Dad said. "I didn't know he was gay."

Saul nodded. "Yeah, few did. He wasn't ashamed, and he and James were quite open about their partnership. But Dudley knew that to live in the country, at least back then—"

"And now sometimes," I interrupted.

"Yeah, now, too. Well, they loved living out here, but they did keep to themselves." Saul ran his hand down his face. "Then James died, colon cancer, and Dudley sort of floundered."

Willie said, "Oh, that's so sad. The house is really lovely. Not necessarily our taste," she continued with a smile, "but beautifully done."

"It was their pride and joy," Saul said. "They would have been great fathers, but ...." He didn't have to finish his sentence. Here in Octonia, a gay couple would have had a hard time adopting a child or even having one through a surrogate. Even now a lot of people would have given them trouble for that.

"I thought he'd moved," Saul said. "Just left because it was too hard to stay." He looked toward the weavers' shed. "I guess not." He glanced at William and then Willie. A long silence settled amongst us. But then, Saul nodded one last time and said, "Where do we start?"

Saul was an incredibly generous and kind person, but he was also someone who liked to keep busy, like my dad. Maybe that's why they'd been friends for decades. Too much talking made them both uncomfortable.

William nodded and pointed to the summer kitchen that I'd just cleared. "Let's start over there. Paisley has already prepped it."

While the Abramses gave Saul the tour, Dad, Lucille, and I moved on to the wagon shed, where we worked quickly and tried to stay ahead of the construction conversation. Fortunately – or unfortunately if you were me and looking to fill your shop with great finds – this shed was relatively empty. We got out a couple of wagon wheels, which could have been two hundred years old or twenty but would still sell. And Dad found a rolling jack that he asked if he could have, per the Abramses' agreement. Somehow in his retirement, he'd decided he would try his hand at changing their oil for the first time. Neither Lucille nor I was thrilled, but I nodded. I wasn't going to try to sell it anyway, and better he learn he'd rather not be a mechanic for free than after costing them a few hundred dollars especially since he might have to foot a hospital bill either way. My dad was not exactly the most safety-conscious guy.

That building cleared, we moved quickly through the garden shed out back and then made our way into the main house, where we made fast work of the few not-original pieces of décor that Willie and William had said we could take. By the time that Saul and the Abramses met us in the upstairs of the house, we had salvaged the few things we needed to get and were ready to load up. "All set," I said. "Saul, you mind if we start filling your truck?"

He took the keys out of his pocket and tossed them to me. "You know the difference between forward and reverse, right?" He winked.

"Thanks," I said with a forced scowl, and the three of us plus William headed down to begin getting all the stuff off the front lawn. "William, maybe you and I can get the old anvil?" Dad, Lucille, and I had barely been able to lift the thing out of the old blacksmith's shop, and while I wasn't that strong, I had no doubt that with the dolly I pushed, William could get the anvil up and over to the truck without a problem. I was absolutely right. He and I – okay, mostly he – were even able to heft the small but extremely weighty thing into Saul's truck bed.

The rest of the items were pretty lightweight, so within minutes, we had the truck loaded and ready to go. The four of us stood around waiting for Willie to finish giving Saul the run-down on the projects for his crew. "They'll start tomorrow?" I asked William while he and I shared the tailgate of the truck and Dad and Lucille wandered around to look at the gardens, taking in each bed and shade level as they strolled. I had no doubt they were planning to offer their help, and the Abramses would be wise to take it. My parents were expert gardeners.

"Yeah, that's the plan," William said, "but I think we're going to have him convert the kitchen into our apartment. You know, considering."

I did know. I wouldn't want to live in the weavers' shed at this point either. "That makes perfect sense," I said. "The space is great, too, and you have that great view down over the stream." The kitchen sat a bit closer to the house than the weavers' shed, and it was also closer to the slope that led down to the floodplain that separated their house from mine. "If you took out a few of those trees, you'd have a perfect view. You could watch the finches in the fall. They come by the hundreds."

"Really?" he said.

"Yep, that's a whole field of wildflowers in the spring and summer. Daisies and coreopsis, echinacea, all kinds. In the late summer and fall, the finches literally descend in flocks. It's beautiful." It was one of my favorite parts of living where I did.

"That sounds amazing." He put a hand on my arm. "Thanks, Paisley. That makes me feel a bit better about our change of plans."

"Of course," I said. "And for what it's worth, I wouldn't want to live in the weavers' shed either." I had a lot of questions about whether or not they'd even turn it into a guest room now, but I decided that was both none of my business and not something that needed to be decided in the moment. No need to put pressure on William.

Saul and Willie came down the stairs, and when they walked over to join us, I hopped off the truck bed. "Well, that's a wrap for me," I said.

"Actually, Paisley," Willie said. "Saul here was telling me you're quite the researcher. I was wondering if we could hire you to gather the history of this place as well as our family genealogies?"

I glanced over at Saul, who just winked. I'd been talking to him about how much I loved writing my newsletter and how, given that the salvage business was pretty steady now, I might want to branch out into more research and such. As always, he was helping me get myself established, just as he'd done with my salvage business.

"I'd love that," I said. "Oh, and I forgot to tell you. My

friend from the clerk's office called. Dudley Davenport owned the property for almost 30 years." I relayed the rest of the information that Trista had shared, and Saul filled in the timeline a bit more precisely by telling us that Dudley had lived here from about 1980 until sometime in 2010 or so. "So if you're sure you want me to do the work, I'll start tomorrow and go back and build out the timeline more, take it back to the land grant if I can."

Willie nodded enthusiastically. "That would be amazing," she said. "Does $40 an hour work?"

I cleared my throat to cover my surprised cough. "Yes, that's great," I said. I had been about to ask for $25, but $40 would mean that I could get ahead on saving for Sawyer's college tuition. Santi and I did fine financially, but we didn't have a lot of extra. These dollars would really help. "Thank you," I said. "I'll come by after I go to the clerk's office and let you know what I find."

Dad and Lucille came around the house, and sure enough, the first thing Dad said was, "Interested in letting a couple old fogies volunteer to tidy up your landscape?" He offered to put together a landscape plan and begin implementing it in exchange for the jack he'd asked for. Soon, all of us were talking about having dinner the next night, and it felt like, maybe, we had managed to lift the pall left by the discovery of Davenport's murder, just a little.

While I wasn't technically scheduled to start my research until the following morning, I could not wait to begin. So once I'd helped Saul and his crew – okay, really his crew – unload the truck at the shop and checked in on my staff who now almost single-handedly ran my store, I headed by the Lafayette to grab myself a burger and fries and then went home to start digging in.

I hadn't done a lot of specific research about a plantation before, but over the past couple of years, I had gotten pretty good at finding information about the places I had salvaged from. While I was most excited about looking into Willie and William's ancestry, I knew that I would have a better grounding for that work if I knew the history of the plantation a bit better first, especially if I was looking to see if their families had ties to the enslaved community there.

Unfortunately, Brown is one of *those* names, the ones that are so ever-present across time and place that it's difficult to research them. Still, I found a couple articles about the "farm" as it was called in the 20th century and their penchant for raising prize-winning angora goats. My favorite photo included a fine white gentleman in a wool suit and fedora standing beside a gorgeous faun-colored goat named, apparently, Bliss. The man in the photo had obviously not done any of the caretaking for that animal – his suit was pristine and wholly inappropriate for working with animals - but he was certainly playing the part of proud owner by placing his hand, almost, on Bliss's head and beaming proudly. The caption said his name was Azrael Brown, and my heart jumped a little. He wouldn't be hard to find in the records. Azrael wasn't that common a name, especially in the pre-Smurf era. He might just be the key that led me to more information about his family and, most importantly, the people they had enslaved.

I spent a couple of hours researching and had been able to put together a tentative family tree for Azrael and his ancestors, all the way back to about 1780, but the further I'd gone back, the more I'd had to rely on other people's research on the genealogy site. I loved having what they'd found available to me as a reference point, but unless they had included specific documents to support the family trees they'd created, I didn't want to rely on them too heavily. We all made mistakes, and building on something I couldn't confirm would just compound theirs with my own. I needed primary source documentation.

As I began to put away my notes and such for the evening, I thought about the oral histories that our local historical society had been collecting and wondered what clues they might give me. Family stories were rich with detail, and I loved hearing them because they told me so much about the people in them. But they weren't documented fact in most cases, and while I valued a good oral history as truth of a very specific sort, it wasn't definitive. However, it might just be reliable enough to get me some leads on where I should dig into the archives. Tonight, I'd gotten enough information to put together a research plan for the clerk's office and headed to the couch for some cross-stitch.

My episodes of *High Potential* depleted, I turned to *The Rookie* and was delighted to see that Nathan Fillion was as charming and funny as ever. But his character was rich with emotion, too, and since he was playing a rookie police officer about my age, I found myself wholly engrossed in the first episode. Finally, though, I picked up my hoop – I was really bad about just leaving my stitching on the hoop despite the fact that I knew it was potentially damaging to the project – and started to fill in the blue book that was in the bottom right-hand corner of the page I'd been working.

The piece was coming together, and I still loved it – but I also realized I had started it when my eyes were younger and not so opposed to 18-count fabric. Now, I had to hold my progressive lenses just right so that I could see the holes for the stitches, even with my bright light above my head. I was grateful, however, to have my glasses since it meant I could also see Nathan's gorgeous face when I looked up. It was a good thing I had decided to embrace getting older because if ever something showed my age, it was how I stitched.

I made it through a couple hundred stitches, finishing up the book portion and moving on to the last rows of the first page. Finally, I could start working on the cat and the sewing machine, the hearts of the project. Now, if Nathan would stop being so funny so that I could concentrate.

I stayed up far later than usual because I was in a rare sewing groove with great entertainment to boot, but by 11:30, I could feel my counting ability failing and packed everything away in my sewing basket so that Beauregard wouldn't destroy my thread overnight. Oddly enough, in a rare show of affection, he came to me as I brushed my teeth and put his front paws up, a request to be held. It was possible the apocalypse was coming because my cat had not done this particular thing since he was a kitten. Still, one does not refuse a fluffy cat who wants to be held, at least not in my house.

With both of us tucked into bed, his head on Santi's pillow next to me, I drifted off into a world of police chases, building-size cross-stitch projects, and a face that kept appearing from a roll of plastic.

I can't say it was the most restful night, especially since Beau decided his brief spate of kindness required a double dose of ornery at 6am. He put his paw on my face, gently at first, but then, when I wasn't responding to his request for breakfast quickly enough, he began to smack me repeatedly on the cheek. The blows were getting slightly more forceful each time, and so I jerked myself upright and away from him. Just in time, too, because as I glowered at him, I saw the tips of white claws just peeking out from his toe beans. "Nasty kitty," I said. "Maybe I just won't feed you this morning. Serves you right."

This statement provoked a long, low growl from my cat, and while I normally operated under the pretense that even when he was grumpy, he loved me and wouldn't really hurt me, that growl was so fierce that I decided not to chance a midnight chest-sitting session that might suffocate me.

"Fine," I said, as I slid my feet into my slippers. "You don't have to be rude."

Beau flicked his tail and preceded me down the stairs, and that tail looked remarkably like a certain middle-fingered gesture that Sawyer had recently learned at school. "Beauregard Sutton. That is not appropriate," I shouted at him. He kept walking.

Some might say I have no standards when it comes to being the leader in my own home. To which I say, "Have you ever met a cat?"

Beau's bowl refilled and my coffee steeping in the French Press, I went to see what I could do with my second-day hair. It was getting grayer and curlier by the inch, and I had recently discovered the value of a great undercut and a high ponytail, especially when I was going to be reading documents. My hair was so thick that if it fell into my eyes, I couldn't see through it, so it had to be out of my face. Plus, I tended to fidget with it when it was down. That kind of fidgeting while I was researching would go unchecked, and I would likely leave the courthouse looking like I'd been elec-trified. Nope, ponytail it was.

By the time I had gotten my hair just curly enough,

washed my face, and headed back to the kitchen for coffee and some steel cut oats, Beauregard was sound asleep with his head upside down in his paw on the chair by the window, soaking in the sunbeam. His life was absolutely brutal. My eyes rolled so hard they almost stuck in the back of my head. It was a good thing I loved him.

Coffee in one to-go mug and oats in another, I headed toward the car. A familiar zing of excitement danced under my skin, and I just wanted to go ahead and get to researching, even if it meant I had to eat at stop signs. Fortunately, the drive into town was pretty quiet at this time of the morning – post school buses and rush hour but pre moms heading to tiny kid things – and by the time I parked by the historic courthouse, I was fortified and ready to go.

The courthouse had been built back in Thomas Jefferson's era, the era by which all things in this region of Virginia were measured, and was constructed from handmade bricks with white columns in the front. The architecture had some unique features – a particularly ornate turned-out corner on the top row of bricks for example, but otherwise, it was what I thought of as a classic early Virginia building. Solid, stoic, formal.

The records room, however, was much more modern with computers for title searches and such, long wooden tables on which the deed books could be spread, and lots of windows that made the reading of old documents a lot easier. With a nod to the woman at the counter, I headed into the records room. Everything in here was available to the public, and most of the other folks working there today were title investigators working for retailers, banks, or lawyers to look at property records. They were always enthusiastic and really good at their jobs, but I could not imagine giving my time to that kind of research. It felt so boring…but then again, most people thought genealogy was boring …so each to their own.

I started with the deeds and looked back through history until I found Azrael Brown and then his father, grandfather, and great-grandfather. At that point, I was working in the early 1700s, and the only information I was going to find earlier than that was a land grant from the king of England. A friend had compiled a map of all the grants in Octonia, so with the modern plat of the Abramses' property in hand, I compared it to the grant map. Sure enough, the Browns had gotten the land directly from the king…without the permission of the Monacan nation who lived there. I took a quiet minute to let that theft affect me, and then I moved on. I'd make sure that the Abramses knew they were living on Monacan land and, if they wanted, connect them to the chief of the nation now so they could talk about what the tribal members might find fitting for a recognition there.

But for now, I had my "starting" point, and I made a list of property exchanges through the years. Next, I went to the will books and begun forcing my way through the absolutely cryptic handwriting on each Brown will I found. Mostly, the wills were full of the usual gifting of land and property to wives and children, but to my very complicated delight, enslaved people were also mentioned in the pages. Azrael Brown's father, Benjamin, had willed "his three boys, Dan, Scipio, and Leon" to Azrael at his death. Then, Benjamin's brother Thomas gives his nephew Azrael, "his woman Martha and her increase" since he didn't have any children of his own.

I quickly started a new list of enslaved people that Azrael Brown had likely owned, and after cross-referencing Benjamin and Thomas's dates of death, I saw that it was likely that Azrael had indeed owned Dan, Scipio, Leon,

Martha, and her children when he built the Abramses' house. That wasn't much information, but it was more than I'd had when I started.

I did a little happy dance in the corner, but when a title researcher gave me a hesitant smile, I straightened up and opened my laptop. I quickly typed in the names listed in the wills, but given that all four of the first names were fairly common, the genealogy site couldn't give me much accurate information. I needed to find more details or more names. In fact, if I could find the names of Martha's children, that would be a great lead.

There was more to research at the clerk's office, but that would wait. I needed to see Xzanthia. Together, she and I could find the next path of research. I quickly slid everything into my backpack, handed the thank you note I'd drafted hastily to the woman at the desk and asked her to give it to Trista, and then walked north on Main Street to the Historical Society.

My friend Xzanthia Nicholas was bending over the long table in the research room when I knocked and then let myself into the old Victorian house that held the historical society. She looked as elegant as ever in a black jumpsuit that fit her tall, lean frame perfectly, and the tortoiseshell glasses perched on her nose gave her an air of quirky sophistication that summed up my friend in all her glory. "Hi," I said. "Whatcha doing?"

Xzanthia looked up and gave me a small smile. In the past, I might have taken her more staid style as apathy or even disdain, but now I knew that was just who she was. She was not going to squeal or stomp her feet in delight, but the fact that she looked up and smiled – that was a warm greeting in her world.

"I'm in the midst of reading a letter sent from a Confederate soldier to his mother. He was at the battle of Manassas and was asking if he could come home," she said as she looked back at the letter.

"He wanted to desert?" I said, my interest suddenly piqued. I was not a military historian by any means, but the fact that someone wanted to leave the Confederacy, that was interesting.

"Yes, he is sick and wounded, and he doesn't believe in the cause of the war either, it appears." Xzanthia leaned down and then made a quick note on a sheet of paper next to the letter. "I'll have to see what else I can find about him."

"I'll be eager to hear what you discover," I said and then sat down at the table. "Do you have some time to do some digging into the Brown place's history with me?"

Xzanthia let her glasses fall on the chain around her neck. "How is that going?" she said as she took a seat across from me. "The salvaging, I mean."

I sighed and quickly filled her in about the discover of Davenport's body and how the Abramses had asked me to do their family genealogies. "I'm starting with the Brown place, though."

"They think their families were enslaved there?" Xzanthia asked.

"They don't know, but I figured that history would at least give them some grounding in their home. And since they want to honor the people who were enslaved there, it felt like a good place to start."

My friend nodded. "It is one of the remnants of the horror of slavery that it's still the white people have to be explored before we can find anything about the black people." She sighed. "Okay, so what do you know?"

I walked Xzanthia through all the research I'd gathered

thus far about the Browns, and I showed her the short list of people Azrael Brown had been willed. "That's as far as I've gotten."

She pulled her laptop toward her from down the table. "Alright, let's see how many people he enslaved in the Slave Census." The genealogy page opened, and she navigated expertly to the right collection before entering Brown's name. "Alright, so in 1850, he is enslaving 37 people, and in 1860, he's enslaving 48." She paused and then said, "That's a pretty significant increase in the years leading up to the war."

I nodded. My limited research had shown me that people began to sell off their slaves in the 1850s as the possibility of war encroached and the resistance to chattel slavery increased. They wanted more liquid cash just in case. But Brown had actually increased his "holdings." That was interesting.

"Alright, so we are looking for, what, four or five families at the Brown place," I asked. Typically, people enslaved families because it made for more stability in their workforce. While families were certainly forcibly separated by sales and the change of residence of their owners, it was typically the desired choice if you wanted your people to work hard for you. Grieving, enraged people are not as efficient. So it was likely that the people at the Brown place were members, by and large, of several family groups.

"That's a good working hypothesis," Xzanthia said. "But these names aren't going to be enough to find our way into that community." She stood up. "We have some Brown family papers here. Let's start there."

I grinned. This is why I had come to the historical society. This tiny nonprofit with only one staff member and a bevy of very committed volunteers was the finest repository of information about Octonia's history in the world, and while they didn't have the cache of the university or state-wide libraries, local historical societies were often the heart's blood of local history.

I followed my friend up the stairs to the collections room, a former bedroom that was full of filing cabinets and shelves, all lined up in rows just like in a library. Only Xzanthia and her most trusted volunteers were actually allowed to look through the collections, a wise move since many of the documents were quite fragile and all were one-of-a-kind. As she made her way to a set of boxes on a shelf near the back wall, I looked around the room at the artifacts set amongst the archival boxes.

On a shelf just at my eye level, there was a large piece of pottery, a crock of some sort with two small handles on each side. It reminded me of the kind of vessels always depicted as containing oil in those Sunday School felt-board presentations we got in elementary school. But this one was squatter and wider.

"What's this?" I said as Xzanthia headed back toward me with a green archival box under each arm.

"Ah, yes, that's actually a really important piece. It's an early 18th century crock from a local plantation, probably used by an enslaved cook." She studied the artifact. "This, though, isn't the original. A fellow from the University made an exact replica for us. The original is stored in a much safer location."

"I was going to say," I replied as I took one of the boxes from her, "that this doesn't seem like the safest location. Just one bump on that shelf . . ."

"Exactly," she said. "Alright, this is what we have on the Browns from your part of the county. Let's go through them."

I followed her back down the stairs and into the research room. We set out our pencils and notebooks and each took a box on either side of the table. "If you don't mind," Xzanthia asked as I opened the lid, "would you mind making notes on each folder so that we can create a finding aid for this collection? It hasn't been done yet, and unless we find something really crucial here, this set of papers isn't set for digitization for a while. I'd at least like to get a finding aid up for people to use."

I nodded. "Of course. That's a great idea. Date, names, short description enough?"

"Yes, and if there are prominent facts or information related to enslaved people, please note that as well."

"You got it," I said and carefully removed the first folder from the box. This kind of research was my favorite because I loved even the most mundane information, like the long letter from a Richmond mercantile assuring Benjamin Brown that his coffee had indeed been sent to him via his neighbor two weeks prior. Apparently, Brown had affronted the shop owner by accusing him of not sending the coffee he paid for. Historical drama was the best.

Now, though, I was very focused on finding the names of enslaved people. Over the years of reading old cursive, I'd gotten pretty good at determining when someone was named – those capital letters stood out – but I still didn't know enough about Octonia family history to be able to distinguish the names of, say, Brown family members from enslaved people. So I began by writing down any first name I found. Later, I'd have to do more Brown family genealogy to sort out who was a family member and who was not, but for now, this system meant I wouldn't miss anything.

Xzanthia was far quicker than I was in this kind of research, and when she gave a little smack to the table and then turned a long list of names toward me so I could read it, I was so glad she was willing to do this kind of research with me – and with the other people who came to research there. She was the expert, and her knowledge always made any research better.

"What is that?" I said as I stood up to lean over and squint down at the paper. My glasses were just not great with that kind of detailed, middle-distance reading.

"It's an inventory," she said, "of enslaved people."

I immediately went around the table to her. "What? Like someone took an inventory of the plantation?"

"Not *like* that, Paisley. Exactly that. Look."

I stared down at the paper and marveled. There, written out exactly the same was the list of plows and butter knives and chickens was a list of human beings' names. A long list. More than a full column on the legal-sized paper. "They listed them exactly as property," I whispered.

"They were property, Paisley." Xzanthia stood back and looked at me. "Is this the first time you've seen a slave inventory?"

I shook my head. "I don't know. Maybe."

She gestured toward the chair behind me. "Sit down. You look a little pekid, green around the gills. I'll get us some tea." She walked out of the room toward the small kitchen at the back of the house.

I leaned forward again and stared at the paper in front of me. It was exactly what it said it was "An Inventory of Property" and yet, there were the names of people, humans. I just stared.

But then, I took a deep breath and forced myself to see past my own horror. If I was incapacitated by the facts of history, I would never been able to share them with anyone else. Instead, I'd be one more white person who made other people's suffering about their inability to stomach it. No, I had to do the work.

I reached over and got my notebook, and then I scanned the list of names. Sure enough, right there in the middle were Leon and Scipio, and there was Dan ...with Martha and their two children, Louisa and Eliza. I sat back as tears came into my eyes. Dan and Martha were married and had two daughters.

When Xzanthia came back with our tea and set it carefully at the other end of the table away from the papers, I was staring into space. "You okay?" she said as she moved toward me.

"I am," I said. "Look." I pointed at the line with the four names I'd just read. "They were a family."

Xzanthia sat down next to me and almost tenderly pulled the paper toward her. "Yes, they were. Wow."

It's hard to explain how momentous that information was, how breathtaking, because now the way we are kin to each other is a matter of public and legal record. But for these people in that time, they had no legal standing, no marriage certificates or death certificates. The best they could hope for is that their owner would document the birth of their children and their own deaths with the local government. But that wasn't a consistent practice, as Xzanthia told me. "This may be the only record that exists of them as a family," she said solemnly.

I looked up at the date on the top of the page: January 1, 1837. Then, I showed Xzanthia the dates for the two wills – one that mentioned Dan and the other Martha. 1818 and 1821. jotted down the dates and then reached across the table for her own laptop, opening the genealogy software as Xzanthia returned to her own computer. For a few minutes, both of us typed and scanned with intent focus.

I tried all the ranges of dates that might work for our family. Dan and Martha had been referred to, in the terminology of the day, as adults – not "boy" or "girl" – so we could fairly safely assume that they had been in at least their late teens when the wills had been written. Given that Martha's "increase" was named but not her children, I also assumed that she hadn't had any children when she was written into Thomas's 1821 will.

It took a few searches, but eventually, I found a census record for 1870 where Dan and Martha Johnson were listed as living in Octonia with their daughter Eliza and her husband, Nat Madison. Dan was 70 years old, and Martha was 66. Eliza was 35, and there were three of her children listed also: Bethy, Joe, and Martha. I let out a soft "whoop" of joy and showed Xzanthia the screen.

"You got it, Paisley," she said. "Three generations. Now, we can find more. You have time?"

"Oh yes," I said. "But can we order some lunch? I'm starving."

While I placed a delivery order for salads from the new café up the street, Xzanthia started building a family tree for the Johnsons, and by the time I sat down again, the three generations of people were on the screen, and the little green leaf icons that indicated record hints were already popping up in the corners.

While Xzanthia followed the genealogical trails on that family, I started working out who else might have been enslaved at the Brown Place. I started with Nat Madison's family, and when I saw that Madisons lived next door to the Johnsons in the 1870 census, I made a guess that the head of the house was Nat's father and began working that line.

Soon enough, I had confirmed that the Madisons and Yanceys were related through marriage as well as being next door neighbors, and soon was I deep into checking all the other people on that page of the census. Two hours later, I didn't have confirmation that the Madisons had also been enslaved by the Browns, but I did have an educated supposition that they and two other families, the Bears and the Spineys, had been enslaved there, too.

"Now, we're getting somewhere," I said as I stood up to stretch. "I can't wait to tell the Abramses."

Xzanthia stood with me. "Can I ask a favor?"

"Of course," I said. "What is it?"

"Could you wait to tell them until I can be there, too? I'd like to meet them and let them know I'm committed to supporting their endeavor."

I smiled. "Absolutely. We're actually having dinner up there tonight with my parents and Uncle Saul. Mika is coming. Would you like to join us?"

Xzanthia's bright smile lit up her face. "That would be lovely. What can I bring?"

We discussed our potluck options for a bit, and then I told her I'd see her at 5:30 at my house. "Casual, Xzanthia," I said as I walked to the front door. "Regular people casual."

She waved a hand at me and laughed.

———

The walk back to my car was remarkably pleasant given the warmness of the day, but still, I was excited for my AC by the time I unlocked the door. I had just lowered myself into the seat and was about to start the engine, when someone knocked on my passenger side door and almost stopped my heart.

I looked over and saw my friend Trista at the window. I

turned on the ignition and rolled down the window. "Tris, you nearly killed me with fright," I said as I forced a laugh.

"I'm sorry, but I've been watching your car for when you came back. I need to tell you something about Dudley Davenport."

Chapter Four

As soon as I unlocked the door, Trista slid into the passenger seat and handed me a piece of paper. "Yesterday, when you called, I knew that Davenport's name sounded familiar, but I couldn't recall why. Thought it was just one of those Octonia things. You know how we all know each other but not really."

"I do know," I said. "I saw someone at the grocery store this morning that we might have gone to high school with, or who could have been a reality TV star. They looked familiar, but I couldn't place them at all."

"Exactly," Trista said. "I didn't think much more about it, though, until this morning when I got your note about your research." She smiled. "Thank you, by the way."

"You're most welcome," I said.

"Anyway," she gave her short blonde bob a little shake. "Your note spurred me to look him up in our full database, and I found that." She nodded toward the piece of paper in my hand.

I unfolded it, and there was a request for a petition for

adoption. I stared at the paper and then looked at Trista and then back at the paper where I saw Dudley Davenport's name as well as the name of a man named James Divers. They wanted to adopt a young girl named Elizabeth here in Octonia. "Whoa," I said as it hit me.

"Right," Trista agreed with a nod. "The petition never went through because James Divers got sick, but it was one of the first adoption petitions I ever received when working for the county.

I stared at the paper a minute more. "Would they have been approved?"

Trista shook her head. "Not then, no. They weren't legally married at that point."

I looked at the date – 2012. "When did same-sex marriage become legal here?" I felt like that was a date I should really know, but I didn't.

"2014," Trista said. "The clerk then just outright denied the petition." She tapped a red stamp of the word "deny" on the bottom of the page. "But in my search, I also found this."

She slid another piece of paper out of her pocket, this one folded in quarters as if she hadn't wanted anyone to see it.

I gasped. "Dudley applied as a single parent to adopt."

Trista nodded. "And look at the name of the adoptee."

"Elizabeth," I whispered. "He still wanted to adopt the little girl."

"Yes, and this time, his petition was approved. He was about to become the father to Elizabeth Russell." She took a deep breath. "But then he disappeared."

I groaned. "He was killed before he could adopt her."

Trista nodded and then held my gaze as if trying to draw the thoughts together in my mind.

Then, it clicked. "He was killed *because* he wanted to adopt her."

"I can't say for sure," Trista said with a sigh. "But it sure looks like it."

Tears pricked my eyes, but I swallowed hard. "Did you call the sheriff's office?"

"Yes," she said. "Forest already came by and got copies of everything." She blushed. "But I knew you'd want to know, too."

I leaned over and hugged my old friend. "Thank you," I said. "I will keep this strictly confidential, but yes, I'm glad I know."

Trista opened the door and stepped out before leaning back in. "We obviously need to let the police do their work, but at some point, I thought the Abramses might like to know, too."

I nodded and smiled. She was right. I started the car as soon as she shut the door. I had a lot to think about before dinner, and I needed air conditioning and my own couch to do it.

The drive home was so familiar to me that I maneuvered it without thinking, which was a mostly good thing because my brain was a bit stupefied by what Trista had shared. I always tried to keep a positive perspective on life, and for the most part, I could, even on hard days. But this kind of thing, it shattered my sense of hope, at least temporarily. Someone wanted to adopt a little girl after the loss of his partner, and in all likelihood, someone else had hated that idea so much that they had killed him before it could happen. They had ended his life and denied that girl a family because of their bigotry. My stomach turned.

When I got inside, I immediately turned on the kettle for tea and settled onto the couch with Beau's favorite blanket because I knew it meant he would get onto my lap. I needed the gentle comfort of his purr at that moment, and he was, thankfully, happy to oblige.

As I sat and petted my massive cat, I took deep breaths, forcing myself to relax a little. I'd get nowhere just letting myself get more wound up by the situation. I needed to just let myself sit with what I'd learned.

By the time the kettle shut off, I was calmer, and Beauregard had reached his capacity as comfort cat. I slid him to the ground just as he began to turn and give his customary hiss of distaste. He sauntered off as if he deserved a standing ovation for kindness, and I went to put a peppermint tea bag, a little half and half, and a spoonful of sugar in my favorite hand-thrown pottery mug, my favorite tea for settling my spirit. I had to pull out all the little luxuries right now to finish settling myself.

After taking a sip of the tea and another deep breath, I sat down at the kitchen table with all my notes and my laptop to review what I'd learned before dinner. I wasn't going to be able to tell anyone about Davenport's pending adoption, so I needed to get my brain focused on the genealogy and such. And by the time I had reviewed everything, had a second cup of tea, and changed into something slightly nicer for dinner, I was ready to give a short rundown on what I'd found and had prepared some questions for Willie and William that might help me follow their ancestors back into Octonia history.

Dad and Lucille arrived about 5:15 with bags of bulbs. "We did our order and got some for you, too," Dad said. I had already planted approximately 15 million daffodils around the property, but I didn't mind having more. Plus, Dad had gotten me a bag of ranunculus, and I was eager to tuck them in next to the summer kitchen out back. "Thank you," I said. "Now we just have to set a date for you to plant them?"

"Nice try," Dad said. "My back no longer does bulb-planting. Actually, I was hoping I could hire Sawyer to plant ours."

I laughed. "Sure, if you're okay with half of them being thrown before going in the ground." My son was one of the most impulsive children, I'd swear, in the world, and while he would really want to help his grandfather, those bulbs were far too ball-like for him to just idly drop them into holes. "Maybe you could make it a shooting contest? Let him toss them from a distance into the ground?"

Lucille nodded. "Now, that's not a bad idea. We'll think about a way to keep him focused." She looked at the scattered papers on the kitchen table. "Find anything?"

"Some things," I said. "Do you mind if I just tell everyone at once? I'd like to get the information to Willie and William first. It's their property."

"Of course," Lucille said. "Alright, I brought you a loaf of bread to take over and a crock of honey butter."

Blood rushed to my face. "Oh my word. I had totally forgotten it was a potluck." I reached over and took the fresh sourdough and butter from her. "Thank you."

I looked over her shoulder and saw Xzanthia and Mika walking toward the house, each of them with a dish in their hands. They had remembered, of course. "Come in," I said as they stepped onto the porch. "We're just getting ready to go."

Within minutes, the five of us were walking toward the Abramses' place, like the five Wise People with our gifts. As Willie opened the door, all of us bowed slightly, as if we had rehearsed, and our host broke out in laughter. "Please, all this formality is not necessary, my people. Come gather as friends." She put on a terrible English accent that made all of us laugh too.

"Thank you, kind lady," Dad said as he stepped through the door with Lucille right behind him.

I stepped up next. "I hope you don't mind. These are my friends Mika and Xzanthia. Xzanthia is the director at the historical society, and she was helping me with research today."

"Nice to meet you both," Willie said. "So glad you're here." Her face was bright, and I was really glad we had organized this together. "Please come put your dishes in the kitchen. We're very informal."

Xzanthia followed after Willie as Mika turned to me and said, "This house is something." She was taking in the wide-board floors and the hand-carved trim. "Wow."

"It is quite a beauty," I said. "And so well-preserved. I'm hoping we're going to find out more about the people who did all this work." I tucked the loaf of bread under my arm and ran my fingers over the perfectly scalloped chair rail that extended down the hallway in front of us.

"I hope so, too. They just don't make them like this anymore," she said quietly.

"No, they don't," William said as he stepped out of a door just a bit further down toward the kitchen. "It's good to be with people who appreciate it. William Abrams," he said as he offered Mika his hand.

"Mika Davis. Thank you for having me." She smiled brightly.

"Any friend of Paisley's is a friend of ours," he said. "Come on through. I'm famished."

Soon enough, we had all filled light-weight bamboo plates with food – fresh kale salad, bread, pork ribs, and the steamed green beans with almonds that Xzanthia had brought. The beautiful rice pudding that Mika had brought for dessert sat in a Bakelite bowl waiting for us to have room for it.

Out behind the house, the Abramses had arranged four small, round patio tables in a larger circle, and then aligned the wrought-iron chairs so that we could all face one another. Saul was already there, a beer in one hand and his face gazing out over the wildflower field below. "Took you all long enough."

Mika rolled her eyes. "Uncle Saul, you've been here all day. Please, enough with the false reprimands." She leaned over and winked at her uncle as she kissed his cheek.

"Alright, you caught me. Beautiful place to spend a day, though," he said as he shifted his chair back toward the table and eyed our plates. "Don't wait for me. I'll be back before you can chew your first bite."

As he headed into the house, the rest of us tucked into our dinner, a meal we obviously completely enjoyed because it was a few minutes before any of us took the time to speak. "These ribs are amazing," I said as I glanced around to see who might take credit for cooking them.

"Well, thank you, Paisley," William said. "I can't cook much, but I can smoke some meat." He grinned and glanced over his shoulder to one of those oval green smokers that so many men loved.

"Oh yes, my husband has been eyeing one of those himself. Perhaps I will now be more enthusiastic about the investment," I said with a laugh. The fascination that many of the men in my life had with grilling and smoking still baffled me. Santi held his own in the kitchen, too, but he was in his element when he was at the grill with a beer and a little music on his phone.

"Well, if he wants to try mine out, he's welcome to

anytime," William said. "Got to get in good with the local sheriff after all." He winked at me.

"Oh, I think hiring his wife for work is probably plenty of a way in," Lucille said. "That man adores Paisley, so if you're good to her, you've already won his favor."

I felt the flush in my cheeks, but I didn't disagree. It had taken me a long time to find a man who was simply good and steady and adoring, and I would always be grateful. "I'll let him know about your offer. I'm sure he'd love to come get some tips."

We chatted about town and the Abramses' plans for the house for a bit, and then, as the conversation lulled, I said, "We did find some information about the people who were enslaved here."

All eyes turned toward me, but I nodded toward Xzanthia. "Would you mind sharing what we found? I think you have a deeper grasp of how it all connects."

Xzanthia nodded and then, to my delight, she stood and said, "We have identified at least two families who were enslaved here around the time the house was built. The Johnsons and the Madisons. Dan and Martha Johnson's daughter Eliza married Nat Madison."

Everyone grew very quiet and still as Xzanthia explained what I'd found in the wills and then what she'd located in the Brown papers. She described how we had put together what we knew and how we thought there was probably a great deal more to find as we continued to research.

"But the best thing I found," she said as she took her phone out of her skinny jeans, "was a photo of Martha Johnson, taken in 1867." She tapped her screen and then handed Willie the phone.

For a long moment, our host just stared at the image,

and then she looked up at Xzanthia. "This woman is my great-grandmother."

Tears welled in my eyes. "Are you serious? You've seen her before."

Without another word, Willie jogged into the house, leaving all of us, even William, glancing at each other in confusion. A few moments later, though, she came back out and handed Xzanthia a framed photograph.

"Well, I'll be," Xzanthia said as she laid her fingers against her heart. "It's her."

"Yes, ma'am, it is," Willie said and taking the photo from Xzanthia, turned it so we could all see. "This is my grandmother's mom. We never knew her last name, but she is Granny Mart to all of us."

I stifled back a small sob, and William stood up to hug his wife, who was now crying. "They found her," she said into his chest. "They found her."

For a long time, we all just sat there, passing the photo of Granny Mart and Xzanthia's phone around and staring at the woman in the images. It wasn't just the same person. It was the exact same photo. The one that Xzanthia had found was much grainier, likely a photo of a photo. But here, Willie had the original, and she knew, without a doubt, it was her great-grandmother.

"Wow," Mika finally said. "Are you okay, Willie?"

Willie and William were seated next to each other, hands interlocked. "Yes, I am. Better than okay." She looked at the house behind her. "The ancestors led me here. I knew there was a pull, a tug that told me this was our house. But I didn't realize it was this clear. My great-grandmother lived and worked here."

"Yes, she did," Xzanthia said. "And now, we can find

out more about her. Tomorrow, may we come by and talk about what you know of her, see what else we can find?"

William nodded. "Of course. Please do, and maybe you and I," he turned to his wife, "can bring out that trunk of family things you have?"

"Yes, let's do that." She looked at everyone gathered. "You are all welcome to come too. I can have breakfast ready at 9."

Saul smiled. "I won't turn down breakfast, but I think my talents are better used in fixing up your family home." He looked at Dad. "You up for a little work tomorrow?"

"Sure," Dad said, and from there, the conversation delved into who would be coming back in the morning to do what. By the time our conversation wound up, the sun was setting, and we were all eager to get a good sleep and come back. All of us except Mika, that is, who had a store to run but promised to do some internet searching of her own to see what else she could find out.

The next morning at 9am sharp, a small group of us gathered on the steps of the Abrams house watching Saul and Dad remove dead stumps and boxwoods from the front yard. They were making quick work of the demolition part of Dad's garden plan, and I was glad to see that they were taking turns using the skid steer to do it. Plus, William was out there doing the heavy lifting and most of the walking as he tugged away the dead wood to the burn pile they had begun in the center of the driveway, away from the tree cover.

Willie had set up a beautiful fruit, eggs, and pastry buffet on the porch, and so while the men worked, the women sat and talked and ate oranges and chocolate croissants. The moment felt very stereotypically southern – the women "gossiping" while the men labored away – but of course, we knew the truth. The men were working hard, but Willie had been up since 6 to get breakfast ready, Lucille had made the chocolate croissants from scratch late last night, and I'd stayed up to the wee hours doing research. Our labor might not be as obvious as the men's, but it was every bit as real and probably more taxing given that we did all we did while also caring for homes and the men in our lives. They were good men, but they were Southern men ...and fourth wave feminism wouldn't reach them for another twenty years probably.

Still, I didn't envy them the physical labor, so when Willie suggested we work in the dining room where the air conditioning was on, I didn't complain at all. Quickly, Xzanthia and I set up our laptops, and Lucille and Willie cleared the breakfast dishes and then joined us, notebooks and pens at the ready.

It was a rare research opportunity because Xzanthia had decided to bring the Brown papers to the Abrams house. Typically, and for very good reason, researchers had to be at the society offices to use their materials. No one wanted anything to go missing or, say, get ruined by a rambunctious six-year-old with a sudden penchant for paper mâché.

But today, the director had decided it was worth the risk to bring both boxes of documents to the house where they, almost completely, had been created. "I don't really believe in things like energy and resonance in terms of history, but something about this situation makes me slightly more inclined to take to heart what so many people call the work of the ancestors," she said when she'd arrived and I'd marveled at the green boxes in her arms.

"I'm with you, Xzanthia," I said. "I don't know what to make of anything beyond the actual work, but I also know better than to discount what so many people see as the voices of their forebears in this research."

"Exactly," Xzanthia said. "And I figure, if they can help, we should facilitate that for them. It's the least we can do."

As we sat at the table, archival boxes, notebooks, and computers at the ready, I looked carefully at all the fine craftsmanship in the room. The ornate crown mouldings and the checkerboard wainscotting made from what looked like oak and cedar that adorned the walls. The beautiful arches that sat above every window, the panes of glass still wavy. This building was a remarkable memorial to the people who had crafted it, and I was honored to have a small part in bringing their stories back to light.

Xzanthia passed one archival box to me and suggested that Willie and I work together as we moved through it. She and Lucille partnered up on the other, and soon the four of us were heads down and deep into the documents. As I had expected, most everything that we hadn't looked at before was commercial correspondence. Planters of this era were businessmen, just like now, and so the use of expensive paper and valuable time were most often dedicated to their financial endeavors.

However, unlike now, planters were often great letter writers, and Azrael Brown and his kin were no different. They wrote letters to family who were in other locations, missives to their friends and colleagues to tell them about their latest agricultural exploits or political choices, and they journaled everything from the temperature and rain amounts every day to how much had been harvested by whom in the wheat fields that week.

When I'd first started this kind of documentary research for my newsletter, I'd readily discounted most of that financial stuff because it wasn't relevant. But then when I joked to a historian about how I was tired of reading how much someone had paid for burlap, he kindly but clearly helped me understand that all that information told us about the time and the situation of the people we were researching. Moreover, he noted that often in this financial correspondence we could find the names of people who were not noted anywhere else – the shop clerks, the delivery drivers, and even sometimes the enslaved workers who carried goods and money back and forth from plantation to mercantile.

So now, even though I personally didn't need all the financial information, I scanned every receipt and ledger entry for names and made notes about the crops and products of the plantation. Willie was particularly interested in the production of the farm since it was now clear her great-grandparents and grandparents even had worked there.

Given that I was more experienced with reading old handwriting on yellowed paper, I took to scanning the documents and then pointing her to the sections about commerce and agriculture when I found them. She then transcribed those portions into a document on my laptop, making her own notes in her notebook as she desired.

Thus far, we'd only really found out the typical stuff about the plantation – they grew corn, wheat, and some soybeans. They raised cattle and sheep, and the skilled craftspeople were hired out around the area to do things like make bricks, blacksmith, or do carpentry for others. The most exciting find was a mention Leon had been hired out to the University of Virginia in the 1840s to work as a body servant for one of the professors there.

"Leon, he's on Benjamin's will," I said and showed Willie the notes I'd made and then the photograph I'd taken of his name. "Let's see what else we can find about him."

I took over at the laptop while Willie carefully started a new page of notes and put Leon's name at the top. Then, she recorded when he was willed to Azrael and then when he worked at UVA. It wasn't much, but even there, we had begun to write a profile of the man's life. It wasn't enough, but it was a shadow of him, more than we'd been able to see before.

For two hours, we continued, researching, noting, sharing what we'd found, including the fact that Leon's last name was probably Johnson as well, and it was likely he was either Dan's brother or first cousin. The names on the census records were overlapping too much for them not to be kin, but we couldn't quite pin down their exact relationship, at least not yet.

All six of us stopped for lunch, pizzas that I insisted on having delivered so that no one had to fuss about cooking or clean-up, and we shared what we'd found in the research. But it was William who got the gold star for the best find. As he'd pulled a dead boxwood out from beside the summer kitchen, he'd seen a lot of glass in the ground. A quick dig with a shovel and hoe revealed it was an old trash heap full of bottles and broken dishes. A *midden* in the formal language of archaeology.

After lunch, we all tromped over to where William had found the artifacts, and for the next hour, we carefully extricated as many bottles, pieces of porcelain, and even a full teacup from the hole. I knew almost nothing beyond what I'd learned in my own previous encounter with a midden some months back, but I suggested the Abramses ask an archaeologist to come do a survey before any more significant digging was done.

While they went inside to make that call, Dad and Saul moved to more manual work, agreeing not to do any significant soil disruption until the archaeologist was on site. And Lucille joined them to plan out where the annual and perennial beds would go. That left Xzanthia and I to go back to the research, and I couldn't wait. The energy of momentum was thrumming through me, and I wanted to see what else we could find.

Unfortunately, the papers revealed very little additional information about the enslaved community. Most of the remainder of the collection was post-bellum and 20th century information, so while we combed through it just to be sure we didn't miss anything, we didn't turn up anything significant.

As I carefully returned my last folder to its box, I said, "Now what? Where else do we look?"

I was a good researcher, I knew that, but Xzanthia was superb. She was already two steps ahead of me. "There are a few of Benjamin, Thomas, and Azrael Brown's papers at the Library of Virginia, but the collection isn't substantial. Probably better if we just hire them to do the research rather than drive all the way to Richmond."

She didn't have to persuade me of that. As much as I loved digging into archives, the hour's drive to downtown Richmond was not something I wanted to take on for a scant chance of information. "Okay," I said. "Any other ideas?"

My friend looked up at me and smiled. "When does your next newsletter come out?"

I tilted my head and smiled back. "Why do you ask?

Chapter Five

I spent the rest of that evening and the next morning carefully crafting my next newsletter to ask people to let me know if they knew of collections of Brown family papers – publicly or privately held – that I might look at. To most people, this request would seem innocuous at worst and very flattering at best, but given that I was looking for information on the people this family enslaved, it was a delicate thing to be both forthright and respectful in such a request.

Some family members would balk at any discussion of their family's slave-holding past, and others would be very eager to make amends if they could – something that some descendants of enslaved people would appreciate and some would not. Feelings and attitudes about the legacy of slavery were vast, and so I had to be very particular in my language as I phrased my article.

Eventually, though, I had a draft, and I sent it off to Xzanthia and the Abramses to get their edits and, ultimately, their approval before I sent it out. They enthusiastically endorsed the letter with Willie and William suggesting they co-sign, an offer I readily accepted. Xzanthia also suggested I include a short write-up on how to donate items to the Octonia Historical Society in case anyone had other materials they wanted to preserve. She gave me the language for the piece, and I slid it in under the main article. Then I attached a quick family tree that I had assembled of the Browns during the 18th and 19th centuries.

I took a deep breath and hit send. Then, I walked away from my laptop and decided I was due a little daytime stitching with *The Rookie*. I rarely had this treat since my work hours were typically quite limited by Sawyer's school schedule, but today, I didn't have anywhere I needed to be. So for two hours, I sewed in the black and white cat on my project and enjoyed police chases and scandals before heading back to the table to begin my research on Willie's family tree.

Willie had emailed her family tree that stretched as far back as her family knew, ending with Granny Mart, five generations back, on her Mom's side and only going back three generations on her dad's. Fortunately, though, her mother had done a lot of the genealogy, so she was able to give me birth dates and death dates for everyone, and even some marriage dates. It was a great start.

Since I knew that Mart had been at their place and the approximate years, I started my search with her, mostly looking at what we knew of the plantation at the time and the people she lived there with. Obviously, we knew her husband and her children, but I was hopeful that perhaps I could find information about her parents or her husband Dan's parents, taking everything back another generation or maybe even two.

As I dug into the research, I lost track of time completely, a situation which wasn't helped by the fact that a bag of chips and the two-liter of seltzer water sat next to me on the table. In fact, it was only that call of the bathroom that made me take a break more than three hours later.

It wasn't typical for me to have such intense focus, not with all the various elements of my job and a young son, but when I could, it felt marvelous, like something got smoothed out in myself, something that I hadn't really known was jumbled up. And the work had paid off, too. I'd been able to find both Mart's and Dan's parents, and while I couldn't get further back in their trees, I knew now that they had both come to the Brown family before they had moved West from Hanover County. So likely, both the Johnsons and the Carters (Mart's family name) had been enslaved by the Browns for many generations. That fact meant that if we could find more Brown papers, we might be able to find out more about her family. My newsletter was crucial.

Since I'd started writing the weekly missives, my readership had grown from mostly people who were interested in salvaged items for their homes, for their interior design clients, or sometimes for resale in their own, higher-end shops to history enthusiasts around the US. I even had a few readers in the UK and Australia. Still, I wasn't sure it was enough.

So I quickly texted Willie to ask her permission, and when it came immediately, I drafted a press release about why we were looking for information on the Brown family and the families they enslaved. I mentioned that I was doing work for a local family with ties to both the Browns and the enslaved community at their plantations in this area. The Browns had owned most of eastern Octonia, and while I was looking specifically for information on the "old place," as lots of folks called it still, it would also be helpful to know as much as we could about all the Brown "holdings" in the area. Plus, asking in general helped keep Willie and William out of the spotlight until they were ready to be in it.

I sent the release to all the local newspapers, to the Charlottesville and Richmond papers, TV and radio stations, and then to a couple of bigger news outlets in DC. I was hoping they'd at least run the press release as an article of sorts in their lifestyle section. But maybe I'd also get an interview out of it, and if someone wanted to do something in-depth, maybe Willie and William would find it advantageous to talk about their plans and families, too. But that would be their call.

I realized, just *after* I hit send on the press release, that I probably should let Forest know what I had just done. Not that I had mentioned Davenport or the murder in anything I'd written, but when that news got out, it wouldn't be long before the locals put together my newsletter, the Abramses, and Davenport's death. It would have been smart for me to consult with Forest first, but I truly hadn't thought of it. Besides, there was some value to the old "beg forgiveness" adage.

But I did want to give him a heads up, so I called him, making rare use of the actual phone feature on my cell, and told him what I'd just written and sent out. He took a long deep breath before he spoke. "Okay, well, we just put out a statement about Davenport's murder. We did not identify the location where the body was found or by whom." He cleared his throat. "Plus, your readers won't necessarily assume that the murder was related to where you were working." His voice got less confident toward the end of that sentence.

"You're right," I said. "But given my *skill* for discovering dead bodies ...." I sighed. "It will take folks about an

73

hour to put it all together instead of a minute," I said. Then, hearing the bite in my voice, I added, "Sorry, Forest."

"Nope, I get it. Believe me, I do. As you know, our community's penchant for knowing just enough about everything to be real trouble makes our jobs here quite hard." He cleared his throat. "You didn't do anything wrong. You were doing your job, and it's kind of you to give me notice. We will handle it." His voice was confident and clear. "No worries, Paisley. No worries."

"Thanks, Forest," I said and hung up. Then, I made myself another cup of coffee because I was going to need it. The proverbial manure was about to hit the gossip-powered fan here in our little part of the world.

By some miracle of the rural life gods, however, by the end of the day, all I had gotten in my email or by text for those people who knew me and took advantage of having my number to be in direct contact, was leads on where or who I might ask about the Brown papers. And when I checked in with Forest, he said that the leads he was getting were only about the murder. "I think our big announcements cancelled each other out in terms of the rumor mill," he joked via text. "Might have to coordinate with you next time."

I chuckled as I put my phone down and continued sorting through the *leads* that I now had. Most of them were recommendations to check places I'd already looked – the special collections library at UVA, the Library of Virginia, etc. But one letter from a woman named Lois looked promising. She said that she knew a living member of the

Brown family through the Daughters of the Confederacy and that she'd ask her about papers.

This was a strong if somewhat ironic possibility since members of the UDC – United Daughters of the Confederacy – were typically history-minded women. Unfortunately, their perspective on history was very, very biased and, I could only assume, quite racist in nature. But still, I didn't need the source of the information to be flawless; I just needed the information.

I immediately wrote Lois back and told her that I'd be so grateful if she would ask and told her that if it would help, I'd be happy to talk with her friend and her about the research. I ended the email with a sincere thanks and decided to call it a night on a high note and go back to my cat stitching and Fillion watching.

I hadn't even managed to close my laptop, though, when an email pinged. It was Lois, inviting me to speak at the UDC meeting at the local library the next day at 11am. "Please be our guest for lunch."

For a long few minutes, I stared at my computer, back hunched and hips screaming as I crouched to read and re-read the message. Yes, she was actually inviting me to a UDC meeting. Tomorrow. For lunch. If it hadn't been for the Confederacy part of the invitation, it would have been a lovely if slightly dated invitation. But that one part, the part where I'd be dining with women who had chosen to gather around the treasonous, hateful perspectives of their ancestors – that stopped me short.

After making myself a pimento cheese sandwich and eating while I paced the kitchen, something I only did when I was agitated but really should have done more often because it annoyed Beauregard to no end. He was due a fair amount of annoyance from me in exchange for all the trouble he gave me. Still, I felt bad for the poor guy who just kept pacing around after me like a duckling, and I eventually sat back down at the table and accepted the invitation.

For the rest of the night, I stitched and stewed over what I was going to say at the luncheon. Was I going to go in hot and tell them I was there out of respect for my clients but not in agreement with anything they stood for? Or was I going to be meek, at least in appearance, and try to gentle more information about the Brown family from the group?

Did I want to take a friend with me for moral support? Was that acceptable? Did I care?

By the time I came to a place of peace about how I was going to approach the next day, I had finished stitching the entire black and white cat and it was 1am. One thing I knew was that I needed as much rest as I could get to be at my best the next day. So I packed up my sewing, turned out the lights, and climbed into bed with my alarm set for 9am.

Unsurprisingly, I was up at 6am and exhausted. While I had slept hard while I slept, as soon as I stirred, my brain – and Beauregard – did, too, and then there was nothing for it but to get up and start the day. Lying in bed while my cat pricked tiny holes in my skin and my brain dervished around wasn't going to bring me more sleep or clarity.

So I got up, cleaned out the coffee from yesterday's late afternoon pot and made some more, extra strong with cinnamon. I had no idea if the claims about cinnamon having anti-inflammatory properties were true, but it wouldn't hurt. Maybe it would even keep my temper in check. Or at least counteract the jolt from the coffee. Maybe.

I kept myself busy by answering emails and entering Sawyer's upcoming school calendar into my own. Then I cleaned the entire kitchen, even behind the mixer, and started the bread machine so that it would be ready when I got home. I was going to need carbs, inflammation be darned.

Finally, I forced myself to shower and get dressed in black slacks and a white blouse. I resisted the urge to put on everything rainbow that I owned and settled on red Mary Janes with chunky heels as my small statement toward non-conformity. Then, I took my laptop and my folder full of notes and drove into town.

The UDC met at our local library in the small conference room upstairs, and since the library was on Main Street, I stopped by Mika's shop to give her a heads up about where I was going. I didn't think I was in danger, at least not physically, but given my lack of sleep, I wouldn't have sworn that I might not start an all-out brawl at the library. I needed someone to be aware of the situation.

"You are going where?" Mika said as I stood in the front of her store with my backpack over my shoulder.

"To the library to have lunch with the Daughters of the Confederacy."

"That's what I thought you said," she quipped. "Why?"

I explained the invitation, the hope that it would lead me to more information about the Browns, and that I firmly believed in building bridges over "some of the divisions in our country." That last reason sounded lofty and a bit arrogant, but it was also somewhat true.

Mika sighed. "Okay, I get it, but you do know that you aren't going to change these women's minds about the fact that what their ancestors did was good, right?"

I stared at her a long minute until she prodded me with

a nod and a stare. "Right." I sighed. One would think that a 50-year-old woman would know from first-hand experience that no one could be talked into changing their perspective. They had to want to change or be forced to. Neither of those was likely this morning. Still, I was an optimist, and as I walked to the library, I thought about that passage from the Bible about seeds on the ground and hoped that at least some of these women were fertile soil.

Most of my hope was destroyed almost immediately when the luncheon meeting began with a pledge of allegiance to the Confederate flag and a singing of "Dixie," both of which I refused to participate in and stood with my mouth pointedly closed for the duration. No one said a word to me about that, though, and after we had all gotten our box lunches and returned to the table, the business of the meeting began.

For the most part, the conversation was about who was going to the national conference the next month and who was applying for membership. Apparently, all the applicants were vetted by the genealogy committee in the group, and from what I could hear over the crunching of my extremely delicious ham and cheese on sourdough baguette, the standards were quite high – direct and documentable lineage from a soldier who fought for the Confederacy or provided aid to the Confederates during the war.

Conversation got heated when one applicant's ancestor had, apparently, signed the Oath of Allegiance to the United States before the official treaty in April 1965 making him, so ironically, a traitor for the Confederate cause. One of the members of the genealogy committee argued that this particular officer had signed the Oath to protect his family but had still fought loyally for the "cause." But others disagreed and said that signing the Oath early was grounds for automatic disqualification.

I listened with fascination both because I felt a bit like I was in a Margaret Atwood novel or some sort of upside-down world but because I rarely heard other people get as excited about history as I did. In some very real way, these women were my people ...but I didn't think any of us was really going to see it that way once I shared why I was there.

Still, the sandwich was good. I loved a free Pepsi, and I was learning both about the UDC and some of Octonia's most prominent families. So far, I was glad I'd come, the pledge notwithstanding. That feeling didn't last long, though, because once the business of the meeting was over, my host Lois introduced me to the group and told everyone about my business and my work to recover Octonia's history. She spoke of me with such genuine appreciation that I briefly considered that maybe these women weren't so bad after all.

But then, the introduction done and a small round of applause finished, I began the thoughts I'd prepared the day before. "I am working with the new owners of one of the Brown plantations here in Octonia, and we are particularly interested in recovering the stories of the people who were enslaved there."

I looked around the room, expecting to see looks of disgust or outright animosity, but most of the women were nodding.

I continued, "So far, we haven't been able to find most of the Brown family papers. I've seen what is available in the public record and at the local historical society, and I've requested some research at the Library of Virginia. But it seems that most of Azrael Brown's papers have not been publicly archived. Might anyone know anything about where I could find them, if they still exist?"

Most of the heads in the room switched from polite nods to stillness or a subtle shake to indicate they had no leads for me. But one woman with a bright red blazer and a gorgeous brooch on her shoulder said, "I'm Bela Brown. I might be able to help." She smiled warmly at me.

"Wow, thank you. Are you related to Azrael?" I looked at her and then to Lois, who was on her right. "I mean directly." Most of the people in Octonia who had been here for generations were kin one way or the other, but some of those folks – like Santiago's Shifflett family – were very clear that they were not "those" Shiffletts or Browns or Massies. Blood ran thick around here but so did memory.

"I am," she said. "Azrael was my four times great-grandfather, and my brother has his papers." Her voice was thin but steady. "If you'd like, I'd be happy to show them to you." She was so genuine and so sweet that I felt disoriented. This had not been the reaction I'd been expecting.

"I'd be thrilled to see them. Thank you," I said, a little afraid to be too effusive with my joy in case there was some catch. "Perhaps we can exchange information after the meeting."

The woman nodded and pulled a card out of her black leather purse.

"Actually," Lois said with a glance toward the president at the head of the table, "I wonder if we might not all like to have Paisley explain how she does her research?"

The president tilted her head and then smiled. "That sounds like an excellent opportunity," she turned to me, "if you're willing, Ms. Sutton."

I swallowed hard. "Well, it's not really up to me, of course. These are Ms. Brown's family papers. She has the power to decide who is allowed to see them." Sweat was pooling in my hands under the table. I was not sure if this turn of events was a good thing or not.

"I'm happy to have Ms. Sutton guide us on how to effectively research with archival documents if she is willing," Bela Brown said with a smile.

"I would be, um, honored," I said and nodded at Bela, then Lois, then the president. "I am, I must say, on a schedule for the research. Is it possible to convene this research endeavor soon?"

The president looked around the room. "Ladies, how many of you are interested in attending?" About 5 or 6 hands went up in addition to Lois and Bela's. "And how many of you are available this afternoon, if Ms. Sutton has the time today?"

I was just taking a sip of my Pepsi and had to spit it into a napkin because of my shock. I looked around, and every hand remained raised. I shouldn't have been surprised. I was the youngest woman in the room by at least ten years. Most of these people were probably retired.

"Alright then, yes, yes, I can do it today." Not for the first time that week, I wished that Sawyer was there. He would have been the perfect excuse to not do what might be a wildly uncomfortable thing. Still, I reminded myself what my friend Mary had told me when I started attending her all-black church. "If you want to be here, Paisley, you have to get comfortable with being uncomfortable." And wow, this afternoon was going to be uncomfortable.

As the meeting adjourned and Bela gave me directions to her house, just up the road from where the Abramses and I lived, in fact, I decided that this gathering was one where I really did need to have some moral support. I hoped Mika had coverage for the store because I was going to need her.

And then, not even two hours later, my best friend and I were standing on the porch of a beautiful craftsman shed, one that I had driven past hundreds of times and admired on each passing. It was a curious house in that it was this style out in the country, but also because, behind it, there loomed a long-abandoned plantation house with pillars and brick arches and all. The yard and house were immaculate with only a hand truck at the side of the porch that looked out of place. I, however, had left a dead fern on my own porch for better than four months, so I wasn't one to judge.

When Bela opened the door, I said, "I have admired your home for a long time." I pointed back down the hill toward my house. "I just live down that way, the blue house by the railroad tracks."

"We are neighbors," Bela said as she pulled me into the house and into a big, bone-crushing hug. She was small but she was strong. "How lovely. And who is this?" Before I could even speak, she was hugging Mika too.

"This is my friend, Mika. She's here to help since she has research experience, too. People might have lots of questions, and I thought it might help if we had two teachers, so to speak."

"Grand idea," Bela said with a flourish of her small hands. "Come in. We're going to set up in the dining room if that's okay with you."

The two of us followed her through an immaculate house decorated with tasteful and brightly colored paintings and sculpture. Clearly, Bela Brown was not a woman who lived into the stereotype of the kitschy senior who collected cat figurines and doilies. Her home was beautiful.

In the dining room, a translucent tote full of papers was sitting on the table, and at each of the 8 chairs that surrounded it, Bela had placed a pencil and a small notebook with her initials *BB* at the top. The sight of the documents and Bela's careful attention to the needs of research made me a little excited about the afternoon. I was still worried, but a little less so now.

"Help yourself to coffee or tea," Bela said as she gestured to a gorgeous oak sideboard that perfectly fit the style of her house. "I suggest we drink in the living room, though."

I smiled. "Good plan," I said and thought how pleased Xzanthia would be to hear about Bela's caution. I had, very briefly, considered inviting her to come along, but I did not think a group of Confederate descendants was a very safe place for a black woman. I wasn't about to put my friend into harm's way, even with a bunch of old ladies.

The rest of the group began arriving shortly after we did, and for a few minutes, we all made small talk with our mugs and teacups before, promptly at 2, Bela said, "Shall we begin?" She set a tray on the coffee table, and we each placed our drinks there and moved into the dining room.

Mika and I had decided on the way over that I would begin this afternoon's workshop – that's what I was calling it anyway – just as I would if I was undertaking this research on my own. So as soon as everyone was seated, I said, "Ms. Brown, can you tell us what you know about these papers?" I tapped the top of the tote lightly.

Bela smiled and nodded. "I don't know much really. My father gave them to me when I started asking questions about our family. At the time, they were just in a big cardboard box, but I could tell they were starting to rip and such. So I moved them to this tote and put the most fragile things into cellophane folders." She looked at me. "Was that right?"

"Yes, perfect," I said. "Do you know who had the papers before your father?"

She shook her head. "I assume his father, but he didn't say." She sighed. "And he's long ago passed away, so I can't ask."

I gave her a soft smile. "I understand. Well, let's get to work," I said with a glance at Mika, who stood up and came beside me as I stood and opened the tote. "The first thing we want to do is organize the materials by date and then by subject. Does everyone feel comfortable helping us with that process?"

All heads bobbed enthusiastically. Mika and I lifted sets of papers out of the tote and began to set small stacks in front of everyone. I quickly jotted decade ranges on index cards I'd brought and lined them up in the center of the table and asked everyone to focus on the dates, setting each document in the appropriate decade.

An hour later, we had the documents all sorted by date, which was really probably the most we could ask for a group of novices to do in terms of organization, especially since they were already lamenting – as did we all – about the terrible handwriting. I did thank them, though, for their help and told them that experience does have its virtues. "They don't teach cursive in most schools anymore, so you can imagine how tough what you just did would be for young people, right?"

This information elicited both laughter and some shock. One woman even vowed to make the return to cursive her crusade in the Octonia schools. If she could do it, I would consider that a successful outcome of the day.

Now, though, we had reached the hard part, the part that was going to require me to explain in more detail what we were actually looking for, the part that I thought would probably bring about the first resistance of the afternoon. I paired the women up so that they could try to read a document together. I moved to the earliest set of papers and took a document and handed it to the first pair of women, Lois and Bela, to my right.

A quick glance told me it was a letter, so I said, "Alright, so here's what would be most helpful, if you're comfortable doing it." Both women were bright eyed and willing. "If you could read this letter, and then transcribe it that would be excellent."

Both of them nodded, and Lois immediately picked up her pencil. They were on-board, but now for the tricky part. "While we want to transcribe the whole document, we are particularly looking for any mentions of enslaved people." When the women simply nodded again, I continued. "So pay particular attention to any first names and mentions of the words *man*, *woman*, *girl*, or *boy* since that's how people often referred to their slaves."

Lois and Bela immediately bent their head to the task, and I distributed documents around the table and encouraging them to do the same. "Remember, the names of people can be on any of these documents," I said when each pair was beginning to work. "So don't discount the value of something like a receipt or account page."

With a deep sense of surprise and a little embarrassment for being so surprised, I watched as these women set to work without hesitation. They quickly decided who would write and who would read, and soon enough, I was beginning to see transcriptions come to life in their flourishing handwriting. I would have to type up the transcripts later, but I didn't mind that. It gave me a chance to read all the documents and, hopefully, facilitate the movement of this collection to the historical society, if Bela was willing.

Mika and I floated around like teachers in a classroom to answer questions and help decipher particularly difficult words or phrases. But after about 20 minutes, the women were cruising along on their own, and Mika and I took our own set of papers and set to work transcribing. An hour later we were all doing that shifting thing that meant our backs and eyes needed a break, and I called for one. Encouraging the women to stand up and stretch, walk around a bit. "You can forget about time when you're doing this, but your body won't," I joked as we all stood and a cacophony of cracking joints filled the room.

I had thought we might lose some of our new researchers after the break, but everyone came back and worked until, at 5pm, I called it. "Women, you have done great work today, and I so appreciate it. But there is a law of diminishing returns that applies to archival research, and we're approaching the threshold here. We don't want to get so tired that we miss things."

A round of sage nods responded to my statement. "But I feel quite confident about you all carrying on with this work as works for Bela's schedule." I looked to our host, who nodded. "Tomorrow at 10, ladies?" she asked and received a warm response.

"If it's okay with you, I'll stop by and see how it's going before lunch," I told Bela and then looked at the rest of the women. "I have to do some other work tomorrow, but I definitely want to see what you find."

And so with a promise of more research tomorrow, we all parted ways after carefully stacking the papers, with acid-free sheets between each decade, on one end of the dining room table for tomorrow. I had two full transcripts and the original documents, taken with Bela's permission, with me in the archival folders, so that was going to be my work for tonight. Or, honestly, maybe the next morning. I was beat.

Mika and I grabbed a pizza and ate it in her shop, tucked into the Cozy Corner where no one could see us from the street. The college student who Mika had recently hired to help out said the store had been steady all day, and the numbers Mika ran after closing seemed to please her. So I hoped the afternoon out had been a good break for her and would give her the confidence to trust this young man with her shop. He was a knitter, and he was good. So if he could also work with customers, she would attract more male customers, and more customers was always a good thing in retail.

The pizza was delicious, but as soon as I had finished my two slices, I headed home, leaving Mika with the clean-up and the leftovers. I felt like that was a fair trade. I was very very curious to see what the two transcriptions – and documents – said, but I was too tired to be very effective at reading anything unless I amped myself up on caffeine again. And that wasn't a good idea.

So instead, I took out my stitching, prayed I wasn't at the end of *The Rookie*, and spent an hour decompressing and getting some of the sewing machine stitched in. But by 9pm, I was ready for sleep and headed up to bed, where I found Beau stretched out like a god on my pillow. I, however, had no patience for selfish gods and quickly booted him to Santi's side. Clearly, it was inferior because Beau huffed and jumped down, probably to sleep on the bathroom floor in a form of inefficient and impotent protest. I, however, did not care and fell asleep as soon as I set my head down on *my* pillow.

The next morning, Beauregard had somehow managed to wheedle his way back onto my pillow next to my head, and when I tried to sit up, he sunk four claws into my skin at the edge of my eye. I carefully extricated myself so as to keep my vision and then unceremoniously plopped him on the floor. "No treats for you," I said as he scowled at me.

Of course, my willpower on depriving him waned as soon as he curled against my legs while I started to read the transcripts, and I tossed him a treat before watching him curl up in a sunbeam across the kitchen. That suited me fine, though, because I really wanted to delve into these documents, even though it didn't look, at least at first glance, like anything related to enslaved people was on the pages.

I didn't get a chance to look hard though because my phone rang shortly after I sat down. "Paisley, this is Willie."

"Hi Willie. What's up?"

"Are you free to come over? Deputy Forest is here, and William isn't. I could use a friend."

I nodded even though she couldn't see me. "I'll be there in five minutes," I said and slipped on my shoes and went out the door.

Willie met me on the porch. "I haven't let him tell me anything because I wasn't sure I could handle it. But apparently, it's something I need to know." Her voice was quiet and fairly calm, but her eyes were wide with concern.

"I'm here, and I can stay as long as you need me." I directed her toward her front door. "Let's go see what he has to say."

Forest was standing at the back windows, looking out over the vista toward my house when we came in. He was in his uniform with his fully loaded belt on his hips. So this was an official call.

"Thank you for waiting, Deputy," Willie said as we walked in. "I hope you understand."

"Completely," he said. "Normally people are asking for a lawyer when they see me, but I can appreciate wanting to have a friend nearby."

Willie stared at him silently for a long minute. "I don't need a lawyer, do I?" she said.

Forest waved a hand and laughed. "No, sorry. That was a joke. No, neither you nor your husband is under suspicion here." He glanced at me with wry smile. "You on the other hand, Paisley . . ."

"Hardy har har," I said. "I've had enough of people being suspicious of me for a lifetime, sir."

He grinned, and beside me, Willie let out a nervous laugh.

Forest grew serious then. "Dudley Davenport has been dead about 15 years, according to the coroner." He took a deep breath. "He had, indeed, been embalmed, and while we can't be conclusive, it didn't appear that his body had been moved in a long time."

I wanted to ask how he knew that information, but I imagined it had to do with something specific about the body itself. I wasn't sure Willie wanted to hear that. Heck, I wasn't even sure I wanted to hear it.

"And he was strangled?" I asked.

Forest nodded. "Looks like by a rope of some sort, something twisted anyway." He started to pull a folder out from under his arm, and I put up a hand.

"We don't need to see photos," I said as I slipped an arm around Willie's shoulders. She was shaking. "What do you need here?" I glanced around at the house.

"I don't think I'll find anything, Ms. Abrams, but I would like to take a look around again, be sure I didn't miss anything." He looked at her carefully. "If that's okay with you. Again, there's no suspicion of your involvement, but it might be that the killer left something here that we didn't know to look for until now."

"A piece of rope a decade old?" I asked.

Forest shrugged and turned back to Willie. "Do you mind?"

"No, not at all," she said. "Anything to help bring justice." She took a deep breath. "Can we help?"

"That's a very kind offer, ma'am, but it's best if I handle this alone." He nodded at both of us and then headed toward the front door. "I'll start with the outbuildings if that's okay."

Willie nodded and watched Forest walk out.

"Paisley," she said as she turned to me, tears in her eyes, "that man's body has been here for a decade. And someone knew it."

Chapter Six

It took Forest a couple of hours to search all the outbuildings, but unfortunately, the renovation that Saul had begun coupled with my salvage efforts disrupted everything too thoroughly for any evidence to remain. "I did a very careful search in the weavers' shed," he told us when he came back covered in dust and cobwebs, "since it was the only building not disturbed. But I didn't find anything except this." He held up a what looked like a piece of red silk tucked inside an evidence bag.

"Is that a piece of fabric from one of the bolts?" I asked as I resisted the urge to touch it.

Forest shook his head. "It's a bowtie. Given that Davenport was in a suit, I expect it fell off when the body was moved." He sighed. "Maybe we'll find DNA or something." He sounded about as hopeful as I felt.

When I looked over at Willie, her face was ashen, and I worried that she might pass out. "Let's go sit down," I said as I took her by the arm.

Forest gave me a quick nod and then headed back out

the door to take the evidence to the station and then, presumably, send it off to the state crime lab for processing. Octonia was resourceful, but we were not wealthy. So all evidence went to the state lab for examination and testing by their equipment. It wasn't a fast process, but it was economically efficient and meant that my husband got to have a deputy instead of a machine he only used once in a while.

As soon as I got Willie seated in the living room, I went to the kitchen and got her a glass of ice water. She took a long swig, and a little color returned to her face. "Thank you," she said after she emptied the glass. "I don't know why that fact about the bowtie affected me so." She swallowed. "All I could see was that tie tight around his neck."

I nodded, letting her follow the train of thought that was already out of the station.

She gasped. "That bowtie might have been what the killer used to strangle him." She drained the last few drops of water from her glass, and I quickly went into the kitchen and refilled it for her.

When I returned, she was staring out the window at the back of the house. She nodded when I gave her the fresh water but didn't say anything further. She didn't have to; I could practically see the spirals of thought and horror circling through her mind.

After a few minutes, I stood and moved to the small card table they had set up in the corner of the room. Their makeshift dining table, it seemed. I had thought to grab my laptop and notes as I rushed out the door, so I set up my station at the table and went back to work. I had been where Willie was, and I knew that she just needed time to process. But she also needed someone else nearby, a reminder that she was safe, that she had support.

As I dug into the emails that had accumulated overnight, I said a little word of gratitude for the fact that I could be this flexible with my work. Lots of folks were tied to offices or in online meetings all day. But I had the freedom to be where I wanted when I wanted, for the most part, and that meant I could still make a living while I supported a friend. It was a good way to live.

Most of the messages that had come in were, of course, offers for sales and discounts at places I had shopped, or thought about shopping. I unsubscribed from most of those so as not to be buried in email every morning, and then I went through the responses to my newsletter. Most were just lovely words of encouragement with suggestions on who might know something about the Browns. Unfortunately, as was often the case in Octonia, the notes were along the lines of, "Have you talked to Sue down at the hardware store? Her third cousin, Stu, used to work up at one of the Brown places on the hill. You know the one. He might know something."

While I made notes about each of these tips, I knew it wasn't likely I would head down to the hardware store to ask for Sue, a woman I didn't know, so that I could ask if she could put me in touch with her cousin who might have worked for the Browns or on a former Brown property at some point. And that's what would be required before I even met Stu let alone found out if he knew anything about Brown papers somewhere. I was all for six degrees of Kevin Bacon-ing it when the lead was promising, but most of these were not.

One email, however, did give me another lead. It was from one of the UDC women, at least that's how she identified herself. She didn't give a name, and she asked me not to reply. "When I was a child, we used to play at the

Brown place that those people just bought up the road from your house. In the attic, we found a hatbox full of old papers. I doubt it's still there, but it might be worth a look."

Well, while not likely that an old hatbox that had been in the attic fifty or sixty years ago was still there, this lead was easy enough to track down, especially since I was sitting beneath that attic right now. I closed my laptop and went over to sit beside Willie, who was now making notes about something on her lap. "I just got a tip that there might be more Brown family papers in your attic. Mind if I take a look?"

Willie blinked a few times but then smiled slowly. "Only if I can come."

"I wouldn't ask to visit a hot, dusty attic in late summer if I wasn't going to hope you'd join me," I said.

"You make it sound so appealing," she said with a small laugh as she stood. "Let's do it."

On our first tour of the house, we had avoided the attic because, even in winter, that space was likely to be 20 degrees warmer than the rest of the house. But in the summer, it would be so warm that we could easily get heat-stroke if we stayed up there too long. I knew that from experience.

Still, I was grateful that it was a full attic with stairs leading up to it. At least it would have a floor and not just rafters. But unlike the attics in more contemporary houses, this one was more than just a dark peak of space. This attic had rooms, and since the roof of the house was hipped, the beams that made up the ceiling were intricate and joined together perfectly with wooden pegs. It was a marvel of architecture.

"Wow," Willie said when we stood in the center of the

large room that made up most of the space. "This is beautiful," she whispered.

I nodded, even as I felt the sweat beginning to slide down my back. "I have a portable air conditioner. I'll go get it and bring it back so we can take a closer look this afternoon."

"Okay," she said, a bit of enthusiasm back in her voice. "But let's look for that hatbox your mystery writer mentioned." She wiped her forehead and then stared at her sweat-covered hand. "Quickly."

We did a cursory look through the space in front of us, but our cellphone flashlights weren't bright enough for us to stare into the shallow corners of the room. A very fast inspection of the small rooms – more like closets – that surrounded the stairwell didn't reveal anything else, and by that time, both of us were not only sweating but panting as well. And I was beginning to feel a little light-headed. Time to go.

The temperature dropped significantly with each step we took down to the main house, and by the time we reached the ground floor, the air conditioning cooled us quickly. Probably too quickly for our good health, so I headed out to the front porch with Willie close behind me. The humid air of the summer day pushed against my face, but while normally, I'd resent that feeling, today I was grateful for it because it stabilized my body temperature a bit.

"You two look like drowned rats," Saul said as he came from around the summer kitchen. "I'll get you water. Don't move." Clearly, we looked pretty rough from our attic adventure.

Neither of us moved while we waited for Saul to come back with glasses of water, and when he did, he cautioned us to drink slowly. "Bring your temperature down bit by bit. You don't want to pass out."

In a few minutes and presumably when we looked like we felt better, Saul said, "Now would you like to tell me what you two women were up to?"

I took a deep breath and said, "Someone told me there was a collection of papers in an old hat box in the attic . . ." I took a breath, but he didn't give me a chance to finish.

"It's probably over 150 degrees up there. It's not safe." He sighed. "I'll get the crew to bring over the portable air conditioner and some lights." He reached for his phone. "But it'll be a while before it's cool enough for you to go up there. Find something else to do."

My instinct was to bristle against his gruff tone, but I knew Saul well enough to understand that the harshness came from concern. "Thank you, Uncle Saul," I said.

Willie nodded. "Yes, thank you."

"You're welcome," he said. "I'll get it all set up. Then, we can go take a look at 3. Do not go up there without me." He turned and walked out the front door, the phone already to his ear.

Willie let out a long slow breath. "We really upset him."

I nodded. "He cares a lot but isn't always the gentlest in showing it." I took another sip of my water. "What do you say to a little road trip?"

Her face noticeably brightened. "I'd love to get out of here for a bit. What do you have in mind?"

I cleared my throat. "Well, I'm not sure you're going to like it."

Fifteen minutes later, both of us were in my car and making the short ride up to Bela Brown's house. "You're sure?" I asked for probably the 50th time as we pulled into her driveway.

"I'm sure, Paisley. I appreciate you telling me who we were going to see, and I am certainly not walking into that house without my armor on. But you don't get to be a 40-year-old black woman in America without being able to take some nonsense." She straightened her shoulders and stepped out of the car.

"I know that," I said quietly as we walked toward the house. "I respect your ability to care for yourself, but I want you to know that if there is any hatefulness, I have your back."

She touched my arm. "Thank you," she said with a small smile. "Let's hope it doesn't come to you having to prove that."

As I knocked on the door, I gave my friend one last look, and when she nodded, I put on a big smile as Bela opened the door even as I internally braced myself.

"Paisley, it's so good to see you," Bela said. "And you brought a friend. How delightful. Come in." I studied her soft face for any hint of distaste or anger, but I saw only a very kind woman inviting us into her home.

Willie didn't hesitate and immediately followed Bela into the house and the back to the dining room, where the UDC women – including two new researchers – were seated at the table, heads bowed over the work.

"Paisley is back," Bela said as she stood at the head of the table. "And she's brought?" Bela looked at me.

"This is Willie Abrams. She's a friend and very interested in this research. We thought we might help and also see what you guys have found." I almost said, "If that suits you," but I was the one who had given them this work. I didn't need their permission.

Every woman looked from me to Willie and then smiled. "Yes, please," Lois said and then stood up. "Willie, is it?" She extended her hand. "It's nice to meet you."

Willie shook her hand and said, "Thank you. Now, where do you want me?"

Bela quickly grabbed a chair from the desk in the living room and slid it between her and Lois. "Will you please work with us? We need fresh eyes."

The three women immediately went back to work on the letter before them, and I slowly made my way around the table and talked with each pair about what they'd found. So far, they'd not found anything substantive – not like the inventory Xzanthia had discovered or the like – but they had managed to record a few more names that likely belonged to enslaved people.

I was just about to settle in with a document of my own when Willie squealed and put a hand over her mouth.

"What is it?" I said, fearing something I couldn't put words too but that felt like maybe Lois or Bela had pinched my friend under the table or something.

"It's Granny Mart," she said and pointed to the document in front of her. "That's her mark."

I stood up and leaned across the table to get a peak at the paper. "Is that a contract?"

"Yes, it is. For work in 1864," Lois said. "Between Azrael Brown and Martha Johnson."

"What?!" I said and gently spun the paper to me. Sure enough, it was a labor contract, signed on January 1, 1864, by Azrael Brown and Martha Johnson and witnessed by two men. "Martha's mark." I put my finger gently over the X that the woman had made to show she agreed since she couldn't write her own name.

"Willie!" I said. "You know what this means?"

Willie's eyes were wide and filled with tears. "Granny Mart was free."

The hubbub of excitement that ensued in the room rivaled the noise of the after-worship coffee hour at church. Everyone was talking at once, and no one could understand each other. But that didn't matter. I could see it in these faces of the women who were still touting the honor of the Confederacy – they were thrilled for Willie. Genuinely thrilled.

After a few minutes of frenzy, the room quieted, and Willie and I read through the document out loud for everyone. "This contract is entered into on first of January 1864 by Azrael Brown and free woman Martha Johnson." As Willie read that her ancestor was free, I heard the catch in her voice, and I was still a bit surprised to see tears in many eyes around the table.

Azrael and Martha contracted for her to work for him as a cook for the term of one year for $12, a sum that was a pittance but actually more than many formerly enslaved people earned in a year. She was also to receive a ration of wheat, corn, bacon, and any vegetables she could grow for herself.

"Have you ever seen anything like this?" one woman asked me.

I nodded. "It looks a lot like the contracts I've seen between former enslavers and newly freed people. A lot of people stayed on at the plantations where they'd worked with contracts like these issued by the Freedmen's Bureau."

The woman looked puzzled. "Why would they stay?"

Willie answered, "Where would they go? They had no

money. No housing. Very few belongings. The plantation was the only place they knew, in all likelihood, and if they stayed, they were paid and got to live in the houses they had occupied as slaves."

The room grew still, and I resisted the urge to drive Willie's point home like a history professor. Instead, I let her words settle into these women's hearts. Right here, in this moment, they were, maybe for the first time, encountering the lived experience of enslavement, of what it stole and what it continued – and continues – to require from the people whose families came out of it.

"And this woman, Martha, she's your ancestor?" another woman asked in almost a whisper.

"Yes," Willie said. "She was my four times great-grand-mother on my mother's side." She cleared her throat. "And now I own the property on which she was enslaved." She took a deep breath and laid her hand on Martha's mark.

An even deeper silence settled in among us, and I closed my eyes, feeling the ancestors of all the women here moving amongst us. We had long history together as people, for better and for worse. But we were kin way back. Land kin through Octonia. Bela and Willie – land kin through the property that both of their families called home.

Bela finally cleared her throat and said, "You bought the place on the bluff?" Her voice was very thin, quiet, and I once again found myself preparing to defend Willie.

"I did. We did," Willie said. "My husband and me. We're going to make it into a hotel."

"You are?" Bela said her voice wavering. "You're going to save it?"

Willie sighed. "We are going to save it," she said. "I'd love your help with that if you'd like."

Now I couldn't keep the tears from streaming down my

face. Here was the repair of history being done in real time. Initiated, with a whole lot of grace and mercy, by the descendant of someone who lived in bondage to the descendant of the person who had held them in bondage. It was beautiful.

Willie extended a hand to Bela, and Bela took it immediately. "I would love that. Thank you."

We were not in the right mindset to research any further, so while the women talked and Willie told everyone about their vision for the hotel as a respite for African American people, I gathered up all the papers, leaving the one with Martha's signature on top. I wanted to scan that for Willie if Bela would allow it. After everything was stacked neatly in the tote and Willie had fomented a new group of volunteer assistants for opening the hotel, I asked Bela if I could take her papers and finish reading and transcribing them.

"Of course, dear," she held my hand in both of hers. "Then, please donate them to the Historical Society. They need to be where people can find them." She turned to Willie. "If you'd like the contract with your great-grandmother's mark on it, please take it."

Willie beamed. "I would love that. I'd love to hang it in the house in a frame. Maybe with a picture of you and I beside it?"

"That would be lovely," Bela said. "Now, I'll see you and your husband for dinner tomorrow night."

Apparently, plans had been made, but I waited until after Willie and I had said our goodbyes and loaded the papers into the car before I asked, "Are you okay?" My friend looked tired but there was a glow to her too.

"I am," she said. "I really am. That was a miracle, Paisley. A flat-out miracle."

I took a deep breath. "Absolutely. I felt the ancestors there."

"Oh yes," she said. "They were with us. Guiding our hearts and our hands."

I paused a moment. "Bela's ancestors, too?"

Willie looked at me. "We all have regrets, some of them bone deep. Yes, them too."

My throat tightened up, and I had to will myself not to cry again as I drove Willie home. In her driveway, I stood up to take the tote of papers out of the back and carry it inside.

She put her hand on my arm. "No, please have Xzanthia preserve these first. I do want that contract, but not until she has a copy for the collection and can tell me how to properly frame it."

I nodded and slid the box back across the seat. "I'll take them to her now. But I will be back at 3 to see what we can find in your attic."

"I can't wait. But first, a nap." She waved as she headed back to the house.

Xzanthia was delighted to get the donation, of course, but it was the story of the UDC women and Willie that she made me tell in the greatest detail. Xzanthia and I had never spoken about her ancestry, and I had never wanted to pry. I didn't then either, but I could see the same sort of sad glow coming from her as I had from Willie. I knew I'd never understand what they felt – and was glad I didn't have to – but it was my honor to witness it.

Immediately, Xzanthia scanned the contract and printed out a photo-realistic copy for the collection. Then, she took out an acid-free folder and slipped the original into it before adding a slip of paper about how to properly frame historic documents. "Here," she said. "For Willie. She needs this back immediately."

"Want to come with me?" I asked as I picked up the folder.

She glanced around the room and, apparently, deciding that whatever was happening here could wait, she said, "Yes, yes I do."

I brought the car from down the street while Xzanthia locked up and put a sign on the door saying she was doing "off-site research." Then, we made our way back over to Willie and William's house. Saul was waiting on the porch with a glass of iced tea when we pulled up, and if he hadn't been covered in cobwebs and sawdust, he would have looked the part of the old plantation owner. Saul, however, would never have bought people to do his work for him. *That's not who Saul is,* I thought.

But as we walked in and greeted Willie, I corrected myself. *That's not who Saul is in 21st century. He might have been that plantation owner back in 1850.* It's one of the things I'd had to come to terms with in all this historical research – the times really do shape the people. A wealthy white man enslaving people in early America would not have been unusual; in fact, it would have been expected. The people who would have seemed "out of line" were those who refused.

My hope was that we were moving forward as human beings, that we would continue to de-normalize the oppression of people who didn't meet typical definitions. But given that Dudley Davenport had been killed because he was gay and wanted to adopt a little girl, it was clear to see we still had a long, long way to go.

Still, I was going to focus on the beauty I'd seen today and leave the ugliness of murder for another time. The world was hard enough without overlooking the really great things.

Saul stood as we came onto the porch, and within minutes, we had rallied Willie and were all heading to the attic. "It's not going to be comfy up there, but we won't all immediately faint," Saul said as we climbed the last flight of stairs to the attic.

I could almost feel his side-eyed glance as we reached the attic door. "It shouldn't take long," I said and pressed down the urge to say that I was as Southern as he was and could take the heat. Obviously, my experience earlier had proved the limits of my Southern temperament when it came to hotboxes.

The attic was, blessedly, cooler. Not cool, as Saul had said, but manageable. And the lights that Saul had set up to shine into all the corners were bright and clear. I immediately saw that one corner just to the right of the stairwell held a jumble of items. I couldn't tell if a hatbox was among them yet, but the possibility felt even more real now.

"There," I said. "Let's get those," I said to Willie as both of us headed in that direction.

"Whoa, there," Saul said. "Hold your horses. There is a floor – I know you're seasoned enough to check for that, Paisley – but we don't know if it holds the weight of a human. Walk on the joists, okay?"

I looked at the wooden floorboards that stretched across the joist and were nailed down. They seemed to be an inch or more thick, quite enough to hold our weight. But I didn't question Saul when it came to construction and buildings. He was the expert.

I nodded and then carefully walked the line toward the

end of the joist I could see sticking out beneath the floor-boards at the edge of the roof. Willie did the same parallel to me, and we were in the corner by the jumble in a minute.

When I was a kid, I'd read all the books where people found grimoires or magical amulets in their attics. I'd watched all of *Charmed*, both the original and the remake, and I knew that the good power in a house often rested in the attic, at least if stories were to be believed.

So when Willie first lifted a small round box out of the pile, I smiled. "That's it," I said.

She gave it a small shake. "I don't think so. Not unless it's a hat for a monkey." She smiled at me. "Besides, it rattles. Papers don't typically do that."

I rolled my eyes. "Okay, maybe I'm a little excited." She passed me the box, and I handed it back to Xzanthia, who had positioned herself halfway between us and the doorway. She then ferried the box back to Saul, who carefully set it on the ground.

For a few minutes we bucket-lined a couple more boxes, a small steamer trunk, and a what looked to either be a haunted house prop or a dress dummy out to the stairs. Finally, the last thing we found was a round box about the size of my upper torso. It was wooden and rimmed with metal on the top and the bottom, and when Willie handed it to me, it felt full but light …just like paper would.

"We found it," she and I said in unison.

Chapter Seven

I impulsively started to lift the box lid as soon as I reached the top of the stairs, but Xzanthia, knowing me well, clamped her hand over mine before I could open it. "Not up here. We need a more clean, comfortable workspace."

"You're right," I sighed and shifted the box in my arms so I could carry it downstairs. The other three grabbed the remaining items, and when we got back to the main floor, we commandeered Willie's makeshift dining table for the "unboxing."

Briefly I thought of making a video for IG like the influencers did, showing the world what we found as we found it. But whatever was in this box wasn't mine to share, not without Bela and Willie's permission. So I kept my phone in my pocket. This was their story to share if they wanted to do so.

I waited for Willie to choose which item she wanted to open, hoping all the while that the hatbox would win. With a wink, she took it from my arms and set it on the table. "Let's see if your source was right."

I grinned and watched as she lifted the box lid and revealed a massive jumble of letters. They weren't grouped or bound up in any way. Just dozens, maybe hundreds of letters in yellowing envelopes with brown writing on the front. Old letters, I could tell right away.

For a long moment, the four of us just stared, and then, Xzanthia said, "Okay, so these are going to be fragile, especially after being in all that heat. Let's go slowly." She reached over and carefully lifted one envelope from the box, sliding her other hand under it to keep it straight as she moved it to the table. "Do you have a dish towel without any nap?" she asked Willie.

"No," Willie said, "But I have a pillowcase. Would that work?"

"Perfect," Xzanthia said as she once again lifted the envelope until Willie returned with a pristine white pillowcase. Once that was spread across the table, Xzanthia set the envelope in its center before sliding a chair over and sitting down.

As she very gingerly opened the envelope, she inhaled deeply and then pulled out the folded piece of paper from inside. The yellowing document was folded first in half and then in thirds, just like I remembered folding letters to my high school boyfriend when he was overseas for the summer.

Next, Xzanthia slowly unfolded the letter and pushed it, gently, to a more flat position next to the envelope on the pillowcase. Only then did she exhale. "This one is in really good shape. Heavy weight paper. If they're all like this, we should be in great to go."

"Should I get more pillowcases?" Willie asked with excitement.

"That would be an excellent idea," Xzanthia said.

"Let's all set up our stations and begin by simply opening what we have here."

Willie headed off toward the stairs, and I sat down, ready to work. Saul smiled. "Alrighty, then, I'm going to head back out and finish up for the day. Unless there's anything more I can do to help."

Xzanthia shook her head as she lifted another envelope out of the box, but I did have an idea. "Do you have the space to check the rest of the attic and see what might be there?"

He grinned. "Yep, a couple of the boys and I will go up and see about anything else that's there. When it's clear, we'll take down the lights, too. No need to heat up the place more…especially with wood that old."

I hadn't even thought about how the heat of those lights might be a fire hazard, but now that he said it, I was even more eager for him to check everything and then return the attic to its dark, sweltering norm.

He was just about to turn and find his men when Xzanthia said, "Actually, I do have a favor if you are going to town."

"Yes, m'lady," Saul said with a slight bow and a smile.

"Are you coming back here after you return to town?" Her face was very serious. "I wouldn't want to put you out."

"I am coming back," he said. "What can I bring you?"

"This key will get you into the historical society building. Would you mind going into the storage closet just below the stairs and bringing me two cases of folders as well as a few dozen cellophane sleeves?" She met Saul's eyes. "Only, though, if it's not any trouble."

Saul blushed, and for the first time ever, he looked a bit flustered. "Not any trouble at all." He took the key from her hand. "Anything else?"

"Perhaps I could text you if I think of something," she said as she held up her phone.

"Of course," Saul said as he typed his number into her contacts. "Anytime."

Then, he turned and headed for the door. Xzanthia immediately returned to opening the envelope before her, and I was left staring because I was pretty sure I had just witnessed the most awkward and formal case of flirting that I had ever seen. I was going to have to ask them about that later. If I could help with a little matchmaking, I was definitely game.

Willie returned a moment later with two more pillow-cases, and soon the three of us were opening envelopes, unfolding letters, and beginning to organize them by date on the sofa that sat just behind us. By the time Saul returned, we had opened more than half the envelopes and had ten piles, all arranged by 19th century decade, laid out around the room. While we had all tacitly agreed that we wouldn't read while we went, I had already gleaned that a lot of these letters were from Azrael Brown himself to a man named Hayward. That would be tonight's research – to determine, first, if Hayward was a first or last name and then to figure out just who this man was.

As soon as Saul deposited the supplies on the floor at Xzanthia's feet, she began to move the sorted letters into folders onto which she quickly penciled the date and the name of the collection – Bela Brown Acquisition. She also took the two very frail letters that we had set aside and slipped them into cellophane sleeves before adding them to the appropriate folder.

Saul headed back out to do one last project down the hill, he told us, and we, by unspoken agreement, went right back to opening the letters. Now that we had the supplies to protect them, it seemed we were all eager to find out exactly what we had here.

Fortunately, as Xzanthia had noted when she began, most of the documents were in quite good shape, so we were able to get everything opened, sorted, and filed in short order. And then, we began with the earliest documents and started reading. It didn't take long for us to figure out that Jarvis Hayward and Azrael Brown had been classmates at William and Mary College, Virginia's first college. Their early correspondence, written mostly in the summer months, pertained mostly to coursework and updates on the mutual friends that they had seen on their time away from school.

But it was the letters post-college, when the men were in their early 20s, that began to take on a different tenor, a more personal one. At first as I read each letter as we circulated them from one to another, I understood that these two men were dear friends. Their letters reminded me of the ones my grandfather had written to his Army buddies, as he had always called them, for decades after the war. There was a connection, an emotional tie between the men that seemed deeper than just normal friendship, something forged, perhaps, in a travail or such.

But by the time, I was on the second decade of letters, I had a new idea burgeoning. I didn't voice it, not until I had something other than just inklings, but I thought perhaps Azrael and Jarvis were lovers. Or if not what we'd call lovers now, at least in love. Since we had letters from both of them, I could see that the declarations of *fidelity* and *loyalty* were mutual and continuous. "I am eager to see you when you pass through Octonia," Azrael wrote in one letter. "We have much to share, and I feel I must lay eyes on you to assure myself that you are not a figment, a phantom hand-writing to me of your fidelity."

That surely did not sound like just friendship to me. Finally, convinced that I was right but lacking written evidence, I broke the rhythm of our reading circle and leapt ahead to the folder with the letters from the 1860s. I noted right away that both men were now writing from Octonia, whereas Jarvis had been in Richmond previously. Even more, their allegiance to each other was intense and ongoing, with pledges of support for everything from business endeavors to disputes that had brought one or the other of them to chancery court. Neither of them ever declared love for the other, but of course, such a declaration, if discovered, might have meant imprisonment or death for one or both men. But these letters got just about as close to romantic as they could be while still allowing a reader to deceive themselves into thinking the men were simply best of friends.

Confident that I was right about Hayward and Brown's relationship, I returned to my seat and cleared my throat loudly. Xzanthia and Willie both looked up, and Willie didn't hesitate. "So they were together, like together together," she said.

Xzanthia nodded. "Is that further confirmed from the later letters, Paisley?" She asked.

I read them a paragraph from one of Hayward's letters to Brown. "Dear Man, I am sorry to be away so long from your company. My business in Alabama has taken longer than I ever imagined, but I hope we will have much time to relate our separate stories one to another when I return within the week."

"I'd say that's confirmed then," Xzanthia said. "Or at

least as certain as we're going to be able to make it from these letters."

"Agreed," I said. "I think it's beautiful," both of my friends nodded, "but in some ways it's not important."

"In others, though, it's the most important thing," Willie said. "Especially given what happened to Dudley Davenport."

I sighed. "Yes, I'm sorry. I didn't mean to imply their love didn't matter, just that it didn't change much about how I perceived Azrael Brown." I stopped as soon as the sentence was out of my mouth. "That's not true. It changes everything, but not because I care he was gay. I care that he was gay in 19th century Virginia. That must have been terrible."

Xzanthia nodded. "I imagine so, but at least they were wealthy planters, both of them. They had the means to spend time together at leisure without stirring up gossip."

"That's true," I said, thinking for the 1 billionth time about what a friend had once told me about how much I could get done in a day if I had just one person doing free labor for me. These men would not have looked out of place on this very front porch, sipping tea and watching the people they enslaved work. I could almost picture it.

Willie shook her head. "Let's not dismiss their suffering, though. The oppression Olympics leaves no one a winner. They were gay men in a time when it was especially dangerous to be gay men. That doesn't excuse their enslaving other human beings, of course, but it also doesn't mean they didn't suffer for who they were." She sighed. "Do you think anyone will look back on our history and see the good we've accomplished? Or do you think they'll only note the way we continue to harm one another?"

"I like to think it'll be both," Xzanthia said as she stood

and stretched backwards. "On my good days, I can think of the early Virginia planter class as people who established our state, who set up our system of government and gave us all the gorgeous landscapes around us. I can remember Thomas Jefferson as forward-thinking and creative, and I can be grateful for James Madison's words in the Constitution, exclusive though they may have been."

I threw my head over the back of the chair. "It is very hard to hold people in their full complexity, especially from a distance. TJ and Jimmy Mad did good things, but they also enslaved hundreds of people." I sighed. "But then I am not all good or all bad either. Or at least I hope people don't expect monochrome choices from me."

"Well, that's it," Xzanthia said as she began to carefully place the folders of letters into piles on the table. "None of us is, as you said, Paisley, one color or the other. Not literally, not figuratively. We are, to quote Uncle Walt, 'multitudes.'"

Willie laughed. "I'd say Walt Whitman is a fitting person to bring into this discussion, given his own life experience."

"Hear, hear," I said as I gathered up the various mugs and cups we'd used throughout the day and took them into Willie's kitchen. "Dishwasher dirty?"

"Yep, just load them up. That was the first thing I replaced when we arrived. I grew up washing dishes by hand, and I am not doing that again," Willie said as she followed behind me with the platter on which she'd put out cheese and crackers. "Thank you."

"No, thank you. What a day, huh?" I began setting the mugs in the dishwasher. "You see your grandmother's mark and we find out that the man who built your house was gay."

Willie chuckled. "I mean, I've always loved history, but it's a whole new thing when it's yours."

"Why do you think I love it?" Xzanthia said. "My family is from here just like yours. All of this is ours. And one of my jobs is to help people remember that. Black history is our history." She gestured to the three of us.

"Yes, ma'am," I said. "Okay, so what are we doing with the letters?" I looked first to Willie and then to Xzanthia.

"Would you like them for the historical society?" Willie asked.

The grin that spread across Xzanthia's face answered the question. "Most definitely, but maybe just quietly for now, until I have a chance to talk to Bela Brown? Technically, they are yours to donate since they were in your home, but I think it would be respectful to talk to her about it first since they are the words of her ancestor."

"Most definitely," Willie agreed. "And maybe we can honor her wishes about who has access to them, at least in the short term, until she determines how she'd like to tell her family about one of their most prominent ancestors."

"And if she doesn't want to tell?" I asked, unable to keep myself from thinking the worst of my new acquaintance.

"Any collection donated to the society becomes part of the public record," Xzanthia said. "So while I wouldn't advertise this romance, it would be available for other researchers to find." She gave me a pointed look.

"Ah, I see. Well, I'd have to think about that, too," I said as I wondered if I could be brave enough to share that in my own newsletter. I hoped I wouldn't be faced with that decision.

"I'll contact Bela tomorrow morning," Xzanthia said. "I need to get her to sign off on the collection she donated, and I will let her know about these letters in as professional but candid manner as I can. Then, I'll let you know, Willie."

"Okay," Willie said. "Can I send you two home with

some dinner? Or would you like to stay?" She was opening the fridge and eyeing the contents.

"I'm beat," I said, "and honestly, peanut butter from the jar with some TV sounds like just what I need tonight. Another time?"

"I must decline, too. I need a shot of whiskey and my bed," Xzanthia added.

"You might need two," Saul quipped as he came into the kitchen. "I think you'd like to see this. All of you."

Without another word, he turned and walked back out the door with the three of us following quickly behind. He pointed at his truck. "Let's drive." Xzanthia climbed into the cab, and Willie and I hoisted ourselves into the bed with the debris that Saul had loaded up to take to the dump.

He drove us past the wagon shed and then down the steep hill toward the road. There, in a patch of newly cleared brush, sat a small white building, about the size of an outhouse. "A pumphouse," I said.

"A what?" Willie asked as we lowered ourselves down from the tailgate.

"A pumphouse. Do you have a well?" I asked.

She paused and looked at me. "I don't know. That's something I should know, isn't it?"

I smiled. "Maybe, but it's just as likely that your water is pumped up from a spring or something. That's how mine works."

We walked the remaining few feet to join Saul and Xzanthia by the building. "Does it still work?"

Saul shook his head. "Nope, it's empty. Doesn't have a modern pump in it at all."

I turned to Willie. "You probably have a well then," I said. "But this building is cool."

Just then, we heard tires on the driveway, and when I

115

looked, I saw a sheriff's vehicle parking. "Forest is back," I said.

"Yeah, I called him," Saul said. "I think this is where Dudley Davenport's body was stored for all those years."

The silence that came upon that patch of land was anything but peaceful, and when Forest came down and saw us all standing around, the tension only got worse. "Did any of you go in?" he said, a rare impatience to his voice.

"No, we didn't," I said. "And we wouldn't have." I put my hand on his arm to calm him. He wasn't usually so easily rattled. That's one of the reason Santi enjoyed working with him so much.

The deputy let out a long sigh. "Sorry. This case is becoming all I can work on. This might be the break we need—"

"And if we had gone in, we might have destroyed evidence or corrupted the scene," I replied. "We get it. We'll just wait by the truck."

Forest gave me a small smile and nod and then turned back to Saul. "Show me?"

The two men walked to the other side of the building from us, and I heard the squeak of old hinges opening. They two of them were talking quietly, but the building walls and the distance were just enough to muffle their voices into nonsensical gibberish. I looked at Xzanthia and Willie, who shrugged, and then I hopped up on Saul's hood to wait.

Saul drove a 1974 Chevy C10 with the original orange paint that had, by some miracle, managed to be nearly perfect despite the fact that he used it as an actual working truck. The hood was steel, and so when my friends joined me up there, it didn't even creak. On my car, the hood would have already caved in.

I lay back against the truck and closed my eyes. Dusk was coming into Octonia, and despite the mosquitoes that seemed to be in excessive abundance down here near the stagnant water in the ditch, the night was still perfect. The air was cooling, and a little breeze was sliding up the hill. I could see Venus twinkling away in the sky above us, and if I let myself dream, I could almost feel the cool of autumn arriving in the air. It was still humid as all get out, but this time of year, the golden flowers seemed to foreshadow the slant of light that came with autumn. A woman could wish anyway.

All hope of the easy days of falls faded away when Forest called me to come over to the pumphouse. "Please don't touch anything," he said and then winced as he registered who he was talking to. "But does that look like the plastic that was around Davenport's body?" He pointed to a jagged scrap in the front corner of the pumphouse, tucked under the two-by-four framing.

I leaned over, careful to keep my balance with my hands on the outside of the building. And then I nodded. "I can't be certain, but it looks like the same kind of thickness. I feel like it's the kind of thing they use to cover hothouses." I'd seen rolls of the same kind of plastic at friends' farms, the back-up they kept if the greenhouse tore.

"Yeah," Forest said. "I think so too. Thanks."

I stepped back as he snapped a few photos with his phone and then reached in with tweezers and grabbed the plastic.

"Is that what made you think Davenport's body had been stored here?" I asked quietly, not wanting to bring up that idea of a dead body to Willie again.

"I actually didn't even see that," Saul replied. "It was

that I noticed." He pointed to what looked to be a pool of lard in the bottom of the cistern.

I swallowed hard. "I don't want to know, do I?"

He shook his head. "I may have to scrub my phone after I googled it."

"You did a Google image search on that?" I said with a shudder.

"Just don't make the same mistake," he said.

Forest walked back over to join us. "Almost certainly this is where the body was stored. Thanks for the heads up, Saul." He sighed. "I don't think we'll get much, but I'll ask the crime scene team to come try for prints and get a sample of the, um, puddle."

"Let's hope this gives you a lead," I said. "Anything come of the adoption situation?"

"Not yet. I haven't even been able to find Elizabeth Russell yet," the deputy sighed.

"She might have changed her name?" I thought for a moment. "Did you look for Elizabeth Davenport?"

Forest squinted. "I did not, but that's not a bad idea. Thanks, Pais." He turned back to the pumphouse. "Okay, I have to seal this building off. Could you let Willie know?"

I nodded. "But how much do you want me to tell her?"

"All she needs to know is that the building is off-limits for now," he said as he started to march up the hill with only a nod at Willie and Xzanthia. He was clearly disturbed. I'd never known Forest not to be up for a little small talk.

I told my friends, in the briefest terms I could, what Forest had said and let Willie know her pumphouse would be locked up for a bit. Since she hadn't known about it before, she said that wasn't a problem. Then, we got Saul to run us back up to the house, and the three of us left for home. I, for one, was absolutely exhausted, and from the weak waves and wan smiles we shared as we drove away, I gathered my friends were, too. It had been a very long day.

At home, I didn't even get the peanut butter out. It was too much work to open the jar and get a spoon. Instead, I opened Sawyer's snack drawer, grabbed a bag of chips, some almonds, and a rogue piece of chocolate and filled my water bottle. Then, I plopped on the couch, texted Santi to tell him I'd had a great but busy day and that I'd fill him in on Sunday, and turned on Mr. Fillion.

He was just in the middle of a high-speed chase ...and then, I woke up to the message about "whether or not I wanted to continue watching." I decided that since Beauregard was sound asleep, he wasn't much interested either and made a mental note to scroll back at least three episodes so I could watch what only my eyelids had seen.

The next morning, I woke up with one of those foggy heads that come from too much brain activity and not enough body motion. I decided to take a walk around the yard with my coffee, just to take advantage of the cool air and get my circulation going a bit. The chickens were happy to see me, especially since they hadn't gotten any treats that week – that was Sawyer's usual chore – and had been living off their everyday feed. I carried out a partially rotten tomato and some strawberry caps and threw them into the run. Just the silliness of their runs for the rotten food gave me joy, and I felt more alert already.

A quick pass by the ever-goldening wildflower field and a glimpse of a great blue heron skirting the creek made the morning walk something I told myself I needed every day. Of course, I had made that commitment before and almost never did it. Still, every time I did, I felt great. And every time I forgot. *Maybe not this time*, I thought as I poured my second cup of coffee and prepared to check email.

The first note in my box was from Xzanthia. "I spent the night reading all the letters. If you can, give me a call at 9. I think you'll want to hear more."

It was 7:45, and I wasn't sure I could wait more than an hour to hear what she'd found. But if she'd been up all night, she didn't need me bothering her so early. I would just have to be patient.

The rest of my email was pretty pedestrian. A couple of people suggesting I talk to the historical society about the Brown papers. I thanked them both and then deleted everything else. Someday I was actually going to unsubscribe from everything I didn't want, but today, I didn't have the stamina. Instead, I decided to shower and go visit Mika at the shop before I met with Xzanthia in person. If what she found was as important as it sounded, I thought I'd want to see the letters myself.

So at 8:30, with a travel mug of coffee, I loaded Beauregard into the car and headed downtown. Mika had been suggesting he would make a great store cat, despite my protests about hair on the merchandise, and he was getting restless with only me to give him homage. I figured today was a good day to see how her idea might work. If it was great, he could spend most weekdays there and snooze in the window. I knew I was always a sucker for an animal in a shop.

Mika was just coming in front her apartment above the shop when I knocked on the front door. She smiled and let me in, carefully locking the door behind me so the early bird yarn enthusiasts wouldn't get in before she was ready. Beau walked in on his leash, looked up at Mika with a single meow, and then headed toward the front window, his leash dragging along behind him. Within seconds, he was curled up and sound asleep in the sun.

"I see my assistant is here for his first day," she said.

"Clearly, he's very nervous about the situation. Go gentle on him," I said.

She laughed and almost petted Beauregard, who, without opening his eyes, let out a low snarl. Mika wisely pulled back. "He seems good."

We walked to the back of the store so Mika could do her opening chores, and I caught her up on yesterday's events. "So needless to say, there's a lot going on."

"I'll say," she replied as she opened the small safe beneath the counter and put the till into the register. "Anything I can help with?"

"I'm not sure," I said. "Probably, but right now, I'm just waiting for word on next steps. I'll let you know." A quick glance at my phone told me it was 8:50, just enough time to walk up to meet Xzanthia. I gave Mika a quick hug, ignored Beauregard, and headed up the street.

Xzanthia was just unlocking the door when I said good morning.

She didn't even slow her motion. "I thought you might just come by. I'm glad," she said as she held the door open behind her for me to follow. "You are going to want to see this."

She efficiently slipped her bags into her office while I waited, and when she emerged with a green archival box, I took it from her. "You've already stored them properly."

She nodded. "It was easy enough to do while I read." She set the box down on the long table in the research room and pulled out a folder near the back of the box. "This is what you'll want to see."

I sat down with the folder in front of me and looked at the ten or twelve letters inside. "Which letter?"

"Actually, it'll be better if you read them all. It'll give you context." She left me then to, presumably, formally open the society to guests. I took out the first letter, slid the folder away from myself and began to read.

It wasn't until I reached the seventh letter that I was sure of what Xzanthia had noted and what had been building through all the letters I'd read so far: Azrael and Jarvis had moved in together when they were both old men.

There, clear as day, "Today, you shall begin residing here," Azrael wrote. "I have waited for decades for this reunion, and now it is almost here."

I sat back and stared at the letter. *Reunion* was an unusual word since the men had obviously been in touch for their entire adult lives. And it wasn't even that Jarvis was moving to Octonia; that had happened a couple decades earlier. No, this reunion was going to be in Azrael's house. I was sure of it.

I finished reading the remaining letters, all sent from Octonia to one or the other of the men when they were away. The location they named was now called "The Homeplace," a name I hadn't seen previously and that made me wonder if it only felt like home to them when they could be in it together.

When I finished the folder, I placed it back in the box at the back, where it belonged by date, and went to find Xzanthia. She was sitting at the small reception desk by the front door. "So you saw it?"

"I did," I said. "And I find it beautiful."

"I do, too," she said. "It felt like the best happy ever after when I read it." Her voice was solemn, though, not very happy at all.

"What's wrong?"

She frowned deeply. "This morning, when I looked up the men's death and burial information, I found this."

She turned her laptop to me, and there, at the top of the newspaper page was the heading, "Local Politician Murdered; Lurid Affair Exposed."

Chapter Eight

I scanned the article as quickly as I could. Killed in his sleep. Knife. Found the next morning by servant. The word that stopped my eyes completely though – *sodomite*. That's what the police posited as a motive.

I had to get my breath and temper my anger before I could even speak. But as soon as I looked up and saw Xzanthia's face, the tears poured down my cheeks. "I can't …."

"I know," she said. "And to think it happened again." She sighed. "I've been trying to find out what happened to Jarvis, but I haven't found anything yet. But this explains why the letters stop so abruptly."

The article was dated 1869, a few months after the last letter from Jarvis to Azrael. "Right," I said, remembering the last letter and wondering why I hadn't considered it was the last letter. "I guess I figured they just were together after that."

"That's what I had been hoping, too," Xzanthia said, "but alas."

"So now what?" I had no idea what to do with this

information. It was most pertinent to Bela, of course, but would she want to know that her great-grandfather had been murdered? Would she want to know why?

"I'm going to call Bela." Xzanthia looked up at me. "Would you mind waiting while I do?"

I nodded. "Of course," I said. "I'll just read some more of their letters, if that's okay."

She nodded as she picked up her phone and began to dial. The expression on her face was almost stricken.

For the few minutes it took Xzanthia to make the call, I feigned that I was reading, but my mind was actually going too fast for me to take in words. Azrael had been murdered. What had happened to Jarvis? Had he died before his husband, lover, boyfriend? What did they call each other? Or did he live on after Azrael was killed? Did he stay in the house or leave?

I began to pace the room, using my body to propel my mind to make the connections I could feel pulling toward each other but still not touching. I resorted to an old technique that had gotten me through college – reciting everything I knew. I started with Azrael's birth and death dates and then Jarvis's. I thought about what I knew about the Abramses' place and about Willie's family, her Granny Mart.

That's when it hit me. Granny Mart had been free in 1864, a strange year to free someone given that the Civil War was raging and people were holding onto the last vestiges of the Old South with all their strength. But that's all we knew. WE didn't know when she'd been freed or why. But we did know that her descendants had continued to work for the Brown family for generations after his death.

I sat down hard in a chair and pulled out my notebook. I made a timeline down the side of the page – 1800 to 1890

– and then I started filling in dates. First I put in Azrael's birth and death and then, after a quick search, filled in the same information for Jarvis, who had lived for at least five years past Azrael and through the next census, where he was listed next to the Johnsons in the record. Likely, then, he had stayed in the house after Azrael had been killed. I got the chills at the thought.

Then, I filled in the dates for Martha and Dan and their descendants. Martha died in 1888 at the age of 84, and her husband passed 10 years before here at the age of 78. Their children live until at least the turn of the 20th century, so I only entered their birth dates.

Then, on the opposite side of the notebook, I made a list of questions.

- When was Martha freed?
- Why was she freed?
- Were her children freed as well?
- How long had she worked for Azrael and then, perhaps, Jarvis?
- Had her children, Eliza and Louisa, also worked for the Browns and Haywards?

None of these answers would bring justice for Azrael Brown or for Dudley Davenport either, but at that point, I just wanted to give someone something. If that person was Willie, then that's what I'd do.

I was just about to dive back into the research about Willie's family when Xzanthia walked in. "Bela would like to see us," she said, her face a shade lighter than usual.

"Was she upset?" I asked as I stood and headed toward my friend. "Are you okay?"

"No, I'm not, but Bela is. She knew about her great-grandfather and his, er, lover. And she knew about the murder." She sighed.

"Okay, then, well, good that you didn't shock her. So what's wrong?"

"She thinks Martha Johnson killed him."

"What? Why would she think that?"

"She says there's something in her grandfather's papers that we need to see." Xzanthia was heading for the door.

"Wait, don't you have his paper here?" I asked, glancing at the tote full of documents that I'd seen waiting in the corner.

"Apparently, she kept something back. A journal."

I hurried out the door after her.

Chapter Nine

On the drive to Bela's, I tried to get Xzanthia to tell me a bit more about what Bela had said, but my friend was resolutely silent after she said, "I think it's best you hear it from her yourself." This did nothing to stave off my anxiety, but I trusted Xzanthia. So I closed my eyes and took deep breaths for the rest of the drive.

When we pulled up in front of Bela's house, she and Lois were standing on the porch, smiling. I looked at Xzanthia, and she lifted her shoulders and shook her head. This reaction was not, at all, what I had been expecting. That disturbed feeling continued when Bela almost ran toward us with a book in her hands. "It's all in here, Paisley. I did what you do and used old documents to solve a murder."

My stomach bottomed out as a slice of this situation snapped into focus. Bela and Lois were trying to solve Azrael's murder ...like I did. I gave them a small smile and turned them back toward the house. I knew they wanted me to be flattered, to feel like they were honoring me in some

128

way, but I just couldn't feel that beyond the utter despair widening like a chasm inside my chest.

"Show us what you found?" I said as they led me toward the house. "I'd like to see." It was the most I could give them in the moment, but they seemed satisfied.

"Yes, come in," Bela said. "Come to the table."

Xzanthia and I set our bags on the couch beside the door and returned to the table, where Willie had earlier made such an amazing discovery. Bela stepped to one long side and invited Xzanthia and I to come beside her while Lois took position across from us. "Show them, Bela," she said as she practically bounced up and down.

"It's right here," Bela said as she laid the book open in front of us. It was a small volume, slightly larger than a woman's wallet and covered in supple gray leather. The pages inside were grayed off and filled with handwriting that I guessed, instantly, was a man's. I'd read enough historic documents to know what the gender norms for script were, and the spiky tops and sharp slant to the letters said a man had probably written this.

Bela opened the book to page with a bookmark with pressed cornflowers on it. "Right here," she said again, pressing her finger into the left-hand page about a third of the way down.

Xzanthia and I leaned forward to read the tiny words, but before we could, Lois blurted out, "She knows. I know she knows. She's a smart woman, and I didn't give her credit before. But she knows. And I cannot have that." She had the pertinent lines memorized. I didn't know what to make of that.

"She knows what?" Xzanthia said as she gestured toward the book, asking Bela's permission to hold it.

Bela handed the book over and said, "About his relationship with Jarvis Hayward. See how this is the beginning of a new entry?" She tapped the date just above the words Lois had shared. "The entries before this are about how he and Jarvis had spent a wonderful few months together in the house. How delightful it had been to see him at breakfast and enjoy reading with him in the evening. How nice it was to have another person to help him make decisions for the farm."

An image of what life must have been like for Azrael and Jarvis started to form in my mind and with it a deepening sense of melancholy. These men had lived together, but if they saw each other at breakfast, that meant they didn't abide together, not as two people in love. Even in their home, they'd had to keep up pretenses of distance. My throat tightened at the very thought.

I took a deep breath and forced myself to focus. I could grieve for these two men later. Right now, I had to figure out what in the history of murder was going on. "Okay, so someone knows about their relationship? I see that."

Xzanthia added. "Tell us more."

Bela nodded and said, "Well, Martha Johnson, Mart as Grandaddy calls her, is the only she that is in this book. She was his housemaid, and she did everything for them. Her husband, Daniel, was the groom and carriage driver, the man who took care of the outside stuff."

I suppressed the eye roll that wanted to come out at the way even enslaved people, who had no choice in their labor, were forced into traditional gender roles about tasks. "Okay, so you're saying the 'she' here is Mart." I resisted adding the word *Granny*, as I now thought of her, out of respect for Willie and her family. That personal term wasn't appropriate when that person was being accused of murder.

"Right," Lois continued. "She figured out that they were a couple, and she killed Azrael because of it."

I looked at Lois and then at Bela before my eyes met Xzanthia's. She looked as stupefied as I felt. "Mind if I sit?" I asked Bela, who nodded and then lowered herself into a chair as did Xzanthia and Lois. "Okay, so walk me through your evidence here. That's what I do for my, er, cases." I did not like that I had developed a reputation for finding bodies and solving murders, but in this situation, it seemed like it might work to our advantage as we tried to figure out what in tarnation was going on here.

Lois and Bela exchanged a glance, but then Lois said, "Well, we told you how the journal is clear that Bela's granddaddy and Jarvis were," she swallowed hard, "together. And then Martha clearly finds out, and Azrael figures out that she knows. He says," she pointed to the quote that she'd shared before, "that he can't allow that. It's right there."

Xzanthia leaned forward. "Ah, so you're saying that he was going to kill her? And so she killed him instead?" Her voice was quiet, and I could see her bracing for the answer.

"Right!" Bela almost shouted. "You get it now."

I sat back in my chair and rubbed my eyes. I was already so tired, and this day looked like it was only going to get harder from here on. I tried to keep my voice even as I said, "But how do you know she was going to kill him?" It felt wisest to explore the erroneous leap in logic first.

Bela looked to Lois, who didn't miss a beat. "Because Martha had a chance to get away from her master and a legitimate excuse for his murder."

Xzanthia put her hand to her mouth in shock but then quickly disguised it as covering a yawn, as if this conversation was the most casual she'd had in a long time. "Alright," she said after a long pause. "But if we're going to actually prove this, we need the direct evidence. We can't make leaps in logic," she glanced at me, "even if they are quite reasonable. That won't hold up." She smiled first at Bela and then Lois.

Bela nodded sagely. "Yes, that's true. We do need that." She looked over at Lois, who looked less convinced. "Okay, how do we get that evidence?"

I cleared my throat. "Well, since we aren't going disrespect your grandaddy and exhume his body, we have to look for clues in the documents. Xzanthia and I will go carefully through the rest of the documents that were in the collection you donated." I looked to Xzanthia who nodded. "And you can comb the journal to make specific notes by date to prove your case. Does that suit?"

Lois still didn't look sold, but she nodded when Bela agreed.

"Start with the dates. Make two timelines. Write down everything on one timeline that you know about your granddaddy's relationship with Jarvis, and then use the other to note anything about Martha's life that you can find." I didn't know if this would bring them any clarity, but I hoped it might just help them see what actually happened.

Xzanthia nodded. "We will do the same, and then we can meet for dinner this evening at the Lafayette to discuss our findings? Does that make sense as a plan for you, Paisley? You're the expert here."

I suppressed my laugh at the absurdity of this statement given Xzanthia's education and vast experience in history, but I knew what she was doing. I needed to be the authority here because these two women had already decided I was. And for other reasons that I didn't want to even give clear internal voice to at the moment.

"That sounds good, doesn't it, Lois?" Bela said with a smile.

Lois looked far less convinced, but she nodded. "Will we be able to publish our case in your newsletter, Paisley?"

Of all the things that these two women had said, that one actually left me speechless, not because I wasn't willing to share my space and audience with others but because I was *not* going to let anyone publish something so baseless as a murder accusation against an enslaved woman, my friend's great-grandmother no less, without very clear proof.

Still, I knew that if we were really going to get to the bottom of this situation, I needed to be sure that I stayed on good terms with Bela and Lois. "Sure. When you get your documentation together, we'll do a full write-up with photos of the documents and everything." I tried to sound enthusiastic, but I must not have gotten all the way there in my tone because Lois squinted at me.

"You don't believe us?" she asked me, and a chill ran down my spine.

"No, I believe you. I see exactly how you came to that conclusion." I smiled. "But before we can share this publicly, we have to have the documents. We don't want you to risk your sparkling reputations or have to spend a ridiculous amount of time fighting with people who don't want to believe you." At this point, I was just trying to protect Willie and her family, but somehow, I must have hit upon the right thing to say because both women nodded sagely.

Bela sighed. "Yes, we know how hard it is to prove truth to people who don't want to see it."

This time, Xzanthia actually snorted, but again, covered it with a cough. "Sorry, I must be coming down with something." She refused to look at me, and I was grateful because I wasn't sure I would be able to hold it together with two

UDC members and their belief that they had been misunderstood all these years.

"It's settled then," I said. "We'll go look through the rest of the documents that weren't transcribed yet, and we'll see you tonight at 6 for dinner."

Bela and Lois nodded. "And we'll dig deep into Grandaddy's journals," Bela said. "And start to make our case." She actually smiled.

But I was stuck on something she said, "Did you say *journals*?"

"Oh yes, this is just one of five," she said. "We might need some of the ladies to help, but I'm sure we can get it done today."

I smiled and held back every concern I had, including the fact that research like this often took a long time, not just a matter of hours. But in this instance, the best thing I could do was just get us out of here so Xzanthia and I could talk. All the things I was holding back were gathering like one of Beauregard's furballs at the back of my throat. "That sounds good," I said as I stood. "See you this evening."

Xzanthia and I walked out the front door and got back into my car. We were halfway down the drive when I couldn't hold back anymore. "What in the holy fire of hell was that?"

"That, my friend, is unchecked racism at work," Xzanthia sighed. "You did well to appeal to their sense of misguided justice, but the irony of their belief system in light of what they are accusing Martha of is almost mind-bending."

I nodded. "Absolutely. Well, are you ready to dig in?"

"I am, but we are going to need help. I'll make a few calls." She was already working through the contacts on her phone.

"Me, too," I said, and immediately voice texted, Mika, Dad, Lucille, Saul, and our friend Mary. This situation required all of us.

Within an hour, everyone we had called, including two of Xzanthia's most trusted volunteers, were gathered at the historical society. Xzanthia and I had set up the as yet unread documents in stacks by decade. Then we'd made ourselves a stack of the documents that the UDC volunteers had transcribed. We needed to see those documents, and as Xzanthia said, we need to be sure that they were transcribed accurately and without bias.

It felt sad that the lovely trust we'd built with those women over the past couple of days might have eroded just as quickly, but if I had to choose where to place my loyalty, it was always, hands-down, with the people whose story has been most erased or revised for the sake of someone else's agenda. I realized, as I began to look at the transcriptions, that the UDC thought this was exactly what had happened with the Civil War, but what people believed and what was fact were sometimes equally powerful in their own minds. But while perception might equal belief, it doesn't equal fact.

Fortunately, the UDC transcribers appeared to have been true to the documents, and while Xzanthia and I continued to spot-check as we read, we weren't finding any major discrepancies in the transcriptions beyond simple spelling errors or misreads. So we were able to read much more quickly and find a few dates to add to our own Jarvis/Azrael and Martha timelines.

We'd asked our friends to do the same as they read,

hoping that the task of looking specifically for those names – or references to "she/her" since they might not name Martha – would simplify things. "Look for capital letters and dates," Xzanthia told them. "We'll read these more thoroughly later, but right now, we need to get this situation sorted."

For a long while, everyone worked diligently, and when I suggested a break, it took each of us a few moments to come out of the focus and flow we'd had when we were reading. The sort of cloudy expression on my dad's face so mirrored my own internal experience of researching that it was a little startling to look at him for a moment.

While everyone else wandered up the street for coffee and pastries, with our order at hand, Xzanthia and I perused everyone's notes. So far, the first mention of Martha had been when she was a little girl of 5 or 6. She helped her mother in the kitchen, and Azrael had written to a friend in Williamsburg saying that he looked like she might make a fine cook herself someday. Just one of those little anecdotes of life, but of course, this one was about determining a child's future for her.

It looked like Azrael had invited Jarvis to move in sometime late in their lives, the late 1850s most likely, but then, Jarvis hadn't actually come until 1860, it seemed. Although Lucille had noted that it seemed he had moved to Octonia in the late 1840s. For twenty years, these men who loved each other had lived in the same town without being able to touch intimately in public. No holding hands, no quick hugs, definitely no kisses. It was profoundly sad.

Still, I couldn't focus there just now. We had an actual mystery to solve, and we had to beat the UDC women to the proof because if we didn't, I imagined they'd use anything they found to prove their perspective, as whack-a-doodle as it was.

By the time our friends and the coffee returned, we had constructed a master timeline on the large flipchart Xzanthia had put on an easel, and we knew roughly the order of events. As everyone sat down, though, I noticed we had a new face in our group. "Forest, what are you doing here?"

"Oh," he said, "I ran into your folks at the coffee shop, and they told me what you were up to. I had been about to call you to ask if you could help me with some history work, but your dad invited me to come along. Said maybe you could all help me." He grinned like the Cheshire cat, and I sighed.

"Alright, well, your situation is obviously most pressing, presuming this is about the Davenport case. How can we help?"

"It is," he said, "and I actually need one of those." He pointed to the flipchart. "A timeline of Dudley Davenport's life. I haven't gotten anywhere with his contemporaries here in Octonia. Nothing stands out as suspicious or even antagonistic. So while I can't rule out that it was one of his neighbors that killed him and hid his body, I need to look more deeply into his past, see if there might have been a lingering grudge."

Xzanthia flipped the page and wrote, "Dudley Davenport" at the top. "What do we know?" she said, her marker poised to write.

Forest gave Xzanthia dates – birth, approximate death, adoption applications, college graduations – any milestone he'd been able to find, Xzanthia wrote on the board. Then I filled in the dates of when Dudley had bought the Abramses house, the two years of unpaid taxes, and that aligned with the estimated date of death almost perfectly.

"Now," Forest continued. "What might have happened earlier in his life to make someone hold a grudge?"

"Oh, is that your only question?" Mary asked. "Totally easy to figure that out." She rolled her eyes at Forest, and he stuck out his tongue.

"Okay, we know a few more things. For instance, he was briefly engaged to a woman." Xzanthia wrote Margaret and the dates of their engagement on the chart.

"So this woman might have resented him for not marrying her?" Dad said.

"Or for getting engaged to her for the wrong reasons?" Mika added.

"Can we start another sheet of possible suspects?" Forest said, and Xzanthia immediately flipped to a new page and wrote, "Suspects" and then "Margaret" below that before returning to the page for Davenport's timeline.

"What else?" Mary said to Forest.

"It appears he had a long-term relationship with another man before he met James." Xzanthia wrote the approximate dates for that relationship on the board.

"Do we know how that ended?" Saul asked.

"Amicably from all I can tell. I spoke to someone who knew both men at the time, and he said they were friends even after their break-up, right until Davenport disappeared in fact."

"So he's not a likely suspect," one of Xzanthia's volunteers said.

"Right," Forest said, "but let's put him on the list anyway. At this point, we need to consider everyone."

Xzanthia wrote the man's name on the suspect list and then spoke to Forest. "Have you located Elizabeth Russell yet?"

Forest shook his head. "No, and I've tried every law enforcement database there is. Nothing."

"Why do you ask, Xzanthia?" I said.

"I don't really like that I think this way, but what if the girl felt slighted because Davenport hadn't gone through with the adoption the first time? Might she have been angry enough to kill him?"

I sighed. She was right, and I didn't like it in the least. "I think we need another sheet of paper," I said.

Xzanthia flipped to a third page and wrote, "Elizabeth Russell." "What do we know about her?" she said, her pen at the ready.

"Not much again," Forest said as he flipped through his notebook. "According to the adoption application, she was 8 years old when they first tried to adopt. And then she was 11 when the second application was filed."

My dad made a couple of notes on a pad of paper and said, "She'd be in her late 20s now."

"Nicknames for Elizabeth can be Liz, or Liza, Eliza, Beth," Lucille added. "So many."

"Do any of you know any Russells?" Mika asked. "I don't."

Every head around the table shook. Russell was just not a common name around Octonia. I hadn't, that I could recall, ever seen it in any of the research I'd done.

"So that's the other mystery, then? Who is Elizabeth Russell now?" Mary said. "Can we even figure that out?"

I glanced down at my watch and saw it was just before noon. "I think I know someone who can help. Shall we order lunch?"

Xzanthia looked at the box still full of pastries and frowned. "We—"

"I'd like to invite Trista to join us. She might be able to

help," I said before Xzanthia could finish her sentence. "And it's only good form to offer someone food when they're taking their lunch break to meet with you."

A smile tugged at one corner of Xzanthia's mouth. "Sandwiches good for everyone?"

"We'll go get them," Lucille said as she picked up her notebook and began to get sandwich orders. I could always count on my stepmom to handle any organizational tasks with aplomb.

I stepped out onto the porch to call Trista, and she picked up on the second ring. "Hey, It's Paisley," I said. "I need your help."

Within twenty minutes, Trista had joined us, and when she walked in, she had a folder full of printouts. "Okay, how can I help?"

I'd given her just the barest overview of what we were looking for, and yet, here she was to help. I loved small town life at moments like this.

Xzanthia and Forest showed her the information we had about Dudley Davenport and Elizabeth Russell, and then the three of them began to look through what she had brought, including new copies of the adoption applications and public records including land plats that came up on a search for the name Russell.

Meanwhile, Dad and Lucille came back with lunch, and we quickly set up a lunch station in the kitchen so that people could grab their food and go eat outside or around the society building, just not near the documents. None of us wanted to push Xzanthia's limits today of all days. She already looked exhausted, and I definitely felt it.

Eventually, Xzanthia led Trista and Forest to the food, and the three of them joined me on the front porch for a few minutes. "Did you figure anything out?"

Xzanthia shook her head. "No, not really. It doesn't look like anyone named Russell who had owned land here had children, at least not with their last name." She sighed.

"And no Russells own land in the county now, I suppose?"

"Nope," Trista said. "That was the first thing I looked for. I did look for someone named Elizabeth Davenport, too, but nothing came up. In fact, the only Davenport in the county, as best I can see, was Dudley Davenport. No one else at all with that name."

"So a dead end with the idea that Elizabeth took his name." I sighed for what felt like the 200th time that day. "How could we possibly find her?"

Forest shook his head. "Short of googling, I'm at a total loss."

"What did you say?" I said, trying to be sure I'd heard him right.

"I said the only thing I can think of now is to Google her." Forest paused after he spoke. "Why didn't I think of that before?"

I shook my head. "Why didn't any of us?" Within seconds, I had a Google search for "Elizabeth Russell" on my phone. The first result was for an actress from the 1930s and 40s, so not her. There was also an audiobook narrator by that name, and an author, too. But while it was possible those were the right person, nothing in their profiles referenced Octonia or even Virginia, so I decided to put them in my mental "maybe" pile and move along. Lots and lots of other references to women by that name came up, but nothing was substantive enough to warrant more investigation. Any of these women could be here, or none of them were. We didn't have enough to go on.

While I'd been tapping away and getting more discouraged, Xzanthia had also been working on her phone. She was very intent, and after a few minutes of typing and expanding screens, she said, "We all need to see this." She got up and went inside.

Everyone else was already back in the research room going through more of their documents, but as soon as Xzanthia turned on the large television above the former fireplace, all eyes were on her. She screencast her phone to the TV, and a newspaper article from the Octonia Gazette in the early 2000s appeared on the screen. The headline ran, "Local girl to play *Annie* in Richmond theater."

"Elizabeth Russell, age 10, was chosen to star in the musical *Annie*, opening at Richmond's Altria Theater in April." I read the opening line several times before scanning the rest of the article and letting my eyes fall on the face of a young African American girl. The caption said, "Octonia native, Russell, to star in classic musical."

For a very long time, the entire room was silent, and then, Lucille spoke. "Well, look at her and her talented self," and the spell of awe broke around the room.

"She was a black girl," I said to the surprise of no one. "Whoa."

Trista whistled. "Man. I bet people didn't like that." She shook her head. "But wow. Dudley Davenport was a rock star."

"Yes, he was," Mary said. "For a single white man to adopt any child is amazing – and I'd imagine rare. But for a gay man to adopt a black child, that is probably in the realm of miraculous."

Xzanthia nodded. "I found several other articles about

Elizabeth, too. She was quite the actress, starring in all the school plays and once in a production over in Barbourton at the theater there."

"Anything about an actress by that name working now?" I said, hoping that maybe Xzanthia was building suspense by dripping out what she'd found.

She shook her head. "No, about the time Davenport died, she disappears from the papers."

"Not surprising," Mika said. "She was a teenager by then, and I imagine she knew Dudley pretty well. The loss must have been devastating." She took a moment. "Or maybe I'm just imagining. Maybe she didn't even know him."

"No, I think she knew him," Trista added. "The only other mention I found of her was in a deposition about Davenport's estate. After he failed to pay taxes on the property for two years, the county did do a search for living family. Someone must have seen the adoption applications because at the time, Elizabeth came forward, claiming to be Davenport's heir."

"Wow," I said, suddenly even sadder than I had been. "What did she say in the deposition?

"The transcript is sealed because she was a minor, but the fact that she was there suggests she probably came forward to say she was intended to be Davenport's heir," Trista said. "But since she wasn't legally named as the rightful heir, even with a Trustee to oversee the inheritance until she was of age, it seems like her claim was dismissed."

"That seems especially cruel," Dad said. "He was going to adopt her. We know that."

Trista sighed, "Alas, the application to adopt is only the first step. The judge would have needed to make it official for the relationship to have any legal standing."

"And Davenport was killed before that could happen," Forest said. "Damn."

I felt much the same way, but words were failing me. Apparently, most of us were feeling the same because the silence stretched into what felt like minutes before anyone spoke.

Xzanthia said, "I fear that we've done all we can do to find Elizabeth Russell."

I plucked at the corners of my mind, hoping I might think of some avenue we hadn't searched, something the professional historian and the police deputy hadn't thought of. But I came up empty. The weight of unknowing weighted heavy. This young woman might be a murderer. She might be a long-lost daughter. But it didn't seem like we'd ever know.

"Thanks for all the help," Forest said. "I'll see if adding any of this new information to the BOLO I put out helps. You never know." I could hear him trying to be positive, but underneath that hope, I could almost fear his frustration. This might well be a murder that could not be solved.

After the deputy left, we returned to our review of the Brown papers. Nothing stood out to any of us about Martha Johnson except that she was, indeed, the cook at the Brown place. But then, just when I was about to call it a day – the fatigue and futility of the search weight me down – Mika stood up and knocked over her chair. "That's it!" she said.

"You found gold," Saul joked. "Eureka is the appropriate term."

She rolled her eyes at her uncle. "No, I know why Martha Johnson was freed."

"You do? Why?" Lucille was standing up now, too.

"She was freed out of gratitude. Azrael Brown freed her as a way to say thank you for protecting him and Jarvis."

"Really?!" I was almost shouting.

"No, Pais, I just made that up." She rolled her eyes my way this time. "Listen to this: 'Dear Jarvis, I have done as we discussed. Martha now has her papers, and I have offered her a handsome wage to stay on with us for as long as she would like. Her, Dan, and the girls as well. They all have their papers, but given that Daniel's injury precludes his former work, he will be reliant on her to manage their financial household. When you return, let us talk to be sure we both feel I have given them a decent wage for both their loyalty and their service.'"

"Holy crap," Mary said, an apt expression for the general feeling in the room. "That is everything."

"Quick, read it," Mika said as she slid the page toward Mary. "Make sure I'm not delusional."

This time I rolled my eyes at Mika, but Mary read and confirmed: Azrael Brown had given Martha Johnson her freedom because she had faithfully kept the secret that he and Jarvis were together. When I put aside the horror of the fact that one human could free another, it was pretty beautiful if honestly the only just thing any enslaver could have done.

Mary briskly but carefully handed the paper off to Xzanthia, who went immediately to the scanner and made a ton of copies. Then, she turned to me. "Let's go see Willie."

I nodded and stood. "I'll text Bela and Lois, too.

They're supposed to be having dinner with the Abramses tonight."

"Okay," Saul said, "but don't tell her what you found until you're there. Make her face the music in front of Martha's granddaughter. That's a bit of poetic justice I think."

"One might even say *reparation*, if one would," Mary added. "Mind if I tag along?"

Soon, Xzanthia, Mika, Mary, and I were on our way up to the Abramses', where Willie had said we were welcome to join them, Bela, and Lois for a casual salad dinner when I'd texted her to ask if we could come by with some great news. "I went a little wild at Whole Foods earlier, so yes, please come help us eat the 25 salads I bought."

I smiled. I'd done the same thing at that store, but in the cheese section. And I hadn't offered to share.

When we arrived, Bela and Lois were sitting with Willie and William on the front porch, all with tall glasses of something sparkling and iced. I hoped it was mint juleps because I could definitely use one but also because it felt like a level of poetic justice that the black people who now owned the big house could serve that super-genteel drink to the descendants of the people who enslaved their ancestors.

Turns out that they were Long Island Iced teas, a fact I learned when I asked about the juleps and had seven people actually guffaw. Apparently, the drinks look nothing alike. I pointed out that my ignorance showed a certain level of restraint on my part, but Mika assured me that it wasn't restraint that kept me from knowing my mixed drinks.

Fortunately, my snafu broke the ice, and by the time we all headed into dinner, Xzanthia with a manila folder of copies of Azrael's letter and me with my pride barely intact, the eight of us were laughing mightily about the various mistakes we'd all made whether it was mispronouncing a word we'd only read – *anemone* was Wiliam's downfall, and we got a good laugh out of the little boy who had loudly read the passage about the sea "ana-moan" out loud to his class.

We all sat down on the porch again with our plates full of every kind of salad from green to ambrosia, which Willie admitted to making since, shocker!, Whole Foods hadn't carried the pistachio pudding, pineapple, and marshmallow delight. And when the conversation fell into a natural lull, I spoke up. "We have great news to share for everyone," I had decided to not humiliate Lois and Bela in front of the Abramses, as much as I felt they were due a little public comeuppance for their racist, biased assumptions about Willie's great-grandmother. "We found out the reason Granny Mart was freed," I said, keeping my eyes on Willie but hoping that one of my friends was watching Bela and Lois for their reaction. I would need the play by play later.

Willie sat up. "Was she his mistress?" Her voice was quiet but resolved. We all knew that such a situation wasn't rare and that on more than one occasion, an enslaver had freed the enslaved woman he'd had a "relationship" with so that his own children with her would be free. And we also all knew that just because someone was gay didn't mean that he wouldn't take advantage of people of the opposite sex if that suited him.

I quickly shook my head. "No, Willie. We found no evidence that Azrael Brown had violated any of the women he enslaved, including your grandmother." I wouldn't swear he hadn't because, of course, it was far harder to prove something didn't happen than it did, but nothing indicated he had done so. "He freed her because she knew he was gay, knew that he and Jarvis were lovers, and she didn't betray their secret."

At this point, everyone was utterly silent, and Xzanthia handed around the copies of the letter for everyone to read themselves. And I finally got a chance to peek at Bela Brown. Her face was beet red, but she was smiling. I couldn't blame her. It was quite a shock.

Lois, however, looked outright appalled. She stared at the letter in her hands, her eyes scanning it as quickly as the handwritten document would allow, and then she said, "I don't believe it" before dropping the paper to the porch floor and stomping on it.

"Pardon me," Xzanthia said as she bent down and picked up the paper. "You might not believe it, but it doesn't make it any less fact. Azrael Brown rewarded a woman who had been loyal to him and who had, at great risk to herself no doubt, protected him and the man he loved." Her voice was knife-sharp, and I was here for it.

"Moreover," Mary said, "he shouldn't have had to have someone protect him for being who he was. But he was fortunate he did." She cleared her throat. "Also, let's be clear. He did an unusual thing freeing Martha Johnson and her family. And by the standards of his time, it was a dangerous and courageous thing. But it was also the only right thing for him to do. And he should have done it for every single person he owned because I guarantee you they all knew."

"Besides, it would have been the only right thing to do anyway." Mika's voice was shaking with righteousness. "No human being has the right to own another human being. Never has. Never will. We fought a war to prove that fact, and if we have to fight another, I'll be joining up."

My friends having covered all the most pertinent points

and successfully cowing Lois, I turned to Willie and said, "Your great-grandmother was a strong and very brave woman. She passed that down to you, and I hope it gives you so much pride to know what kind of person she was."

Willie was crying, and she nodded. "It does. It absolutely does." She looked, then, past Lois to Bela. "Your grandfather treated my grandmother well, and while we will have to work hard to overcome the way history has divided us, I hope we will continue to do so and become dear friends. This place is always open to you. Anytime."

Bela swallowed hard and said a quiet "Thank you" before standing up and saying, "We best be going. Forgive us for not staying to help you clean up." She and Lois then went down the stairs and were in her massive pick-up truck within a minute, not another word said to anyone.

For a brief moment, I thought we were going to let those two women destroy this beautiful moment, but Xzanthia wasn't going to have that. "We will deal with them later. They do not get to steal your light," she said to Willie as soon as their car was out of sight. "Tonight, we are celebrating Martha Johnson and her courage."

"With mint juleps," William said with a wink at me. "Paisley and Mika, come help me make them. Mika, we can teach this liquor novice a thing or two."

The two of us followed William inside, and as I turned to look back, Xzanthia and Mary had come to sit beside Willie in the way, I imagined, black women had always done for one another. It was, I believed, the reason that so many people had survived through slavery – the strength of black women holding them up.

But the intensity of the revelation passed as soon as we walked back out with two mint juleps each. From then on, it was just a wonderful celebration on a late summer Friday night on the porch of a house where justice had been served 160 years ago …and was coming to light now. With mint at its back.

I had planned on spending the entire day before Santi and Sawyer returned sewing and watching TV, maybe cleaning if I got really motivated. But when Xzanthia suggested, as we left the Abramses late in the evening, that we finish reading Azrael Brown's papers, I didn't hesitate.

After Bela Brown's decision to blame Martha Johnson for her great-grandfather's death, lack of evidence withstanding, Xzanthia had decided to just have Willie give her the letters between Azrael and Jarvis. They were legally Willie and William's property, and now, she didn't feel inclined to give Bela the courtesy of a say in the matter. So she'd had Willie sign the transfer of documents, and now, the historical society had an excellent collection of Azrael Brown's papers for its archives.

And the public could access all of them, once they were cataloged. So that was a top priority, especially given that the headline of the Octonia Gazette this morning had been, "Local Man's Body Found Ten Years Later." The news about Davenport's death had finally leaked, and there was no doubt we were going to get a lot of questions.

When I arrived at the historical society with coffee, chocolate croissants, and Mika at 9am sharp, Xzanthia was already on the phone. "No, we don't have any of Mr. Davenport's papers. No, we don't have a statement on his death. Thank you." She hung up.

"Might I suggest you let voicemail get the rest of those today?" Mika said as she handed over an extra-large cup of black coffee.

"I will gladly take that suggestion," Xzanthia said before turning off the landline's ringer and sipping her coffee. "I must say, though, I slept soundly last night. It's a wonder what a little justice can do to settle one's mind." She was outright gloating, and it was a look I liked on my usually serene, almost stoic friend.

"Same," I said. "After I settled with some stitching in silence. I can no longer go to bed with any hope of sleep if I'm still wired. Fortunately, between the mint julep and cross-stitch, I was in bed by 10."

A moment later, the door to the society opened, and Mary came in, carrying a huge fruit salad and bread that still smelled like it was baking. "At least one of us thought to bring coffee," she said as she set the food and a small circle of paper plates in the kitchen. "Might I be so bold as to—?"

I thrust another large cup into her hands. "Two creams, three sugars."

"Bless you, child," Mary said and smelled the coffee. "I needed this."

"Well drink up. We have lots of work to do," Xzanthia said as she headed toward the kitchen for breakfast.

For the rest of the morning, the four of us read our way through all the unread papers in the collection Bela Brown had donated. "Thank goodness she already signed these over," Mary said at one point. "I doubt she'd do that now."

I had to agree, and the thought unsettled me. Bela had seemed so open to understanding her family in a new way just a couple of days ago. But yesterday, it's as if any insight she'd gained had been turned off like a light. I knew that it was hard for people to change their deeply held beliefs – I had challenges there myself – but to begin to change and then just revert so quickly.

"It's her great-grandfather," Mary said gently when I aired my thoughts in the room. "It's one thing to come to a more pleasing picture of him as the 'good master,'" she made air quotes, "but it's another entirely to honestly contend with his death. It's really no wonder she jumped to the conclusion she did, as horrible as it was, because it kept her grandfather the hero and kept Martha in her place."

"When you put it like that…" I replied. The thought stole a bit of the hopefulness I'd been feeling since last night.

After ordering Chinese food for lunch, we moved onto what Xzanthia called, "Stage 2" of the archiving process – the actual organization of the documents by type and then author for letters. Given that at least one of us had now read everything in the collection, this part went fairly quickly, and by mid-afternoon, we had neatly sorted piles of documents that we put into new archival folders (Xzanthia recycled the old ones for business files).

"The last step, then, is to create a finding aid. I would suggest that Paisley and Mika do Azrael and Jarvis' letters since those are already sufficiently organized by date, and Mary and I will do the more various collection." Xzanthia was fully in director mode, and I was reminded just how great she was at her job.

We had just set down to work at opposite ends of the table in the research room when my phone rang. The number was local but unknown. Normally, I would have just let it go to voicemail, but given the events of the last few days, I decided to answer. Lois was on the line and shrieking.

I pulled the phone away from my ear, set it on the table, and tapped the speaker button. Normally I'd tell someone they were on speaker and who was in the room, but Lois wasn't stopping for breath. "I cannot believe you," she was saying. "You took *their* side," she said. "How can you possibly believe them after all the lies they've told about slavery? Azrael Brown was a good master."

Mary had to slap her hand over her mouth to keep from laughing, and I didn't blame her. This was classic neo-Confederate nonsense, and since we'd all grown up here in Virginia, heart of the Confederacy, we were far too familiar with the rhetoric. We were also well aware that trying to argue for the truth when someone was this worked up wasn't a valuable use of our time at best and might have been actually dangerous at worst. So I let her continue her tirade, while the four of us went back to work.

Eventually, Lois blustered out, and I was able to say my first word. "Lois, before you continue, I want you to know that you are on speaker phone with me, Xzanthia, Mika, and Mary." I paused to give her a moment to take that in and, hope against hope, apologize. She did not.

"Good, I want them to hear this too. What you have done to Bela Brown is nothing less than unconscionable. She is a wreck, and it's your fault." Lois's voice was climbing in tenor and pitch again.

"Lois, I'm going to stop you right there," I said, recalling an Elyse Myers video on Facebook about the first time she had learned to not let someone's hatefulness affect her. "We do not accept your blame or your vitriol. Either you can speak kindly and calmly, or this conversation is over."

Mary signed applause in ASL, and Mika gave me a thumbs up. Xzanthia didn't even bother to look at anyone. She just kept working.

My words must have stunned Lois into silence because there was just a long pause of open air on the line. Then, she said, "I apologize for my tone."

I sighed. A classic white person, particularly a Southern white person, ploy. Policing tone, even our own, made us feel like we were actually contrite when what we were actually doing was reinforcing civility instead of actually allowing ourselves the room to change.

"Is there anything else, Lois?" I said, sitting down and preparing to hold my boundary about kindness. I felt pretty proud that I managed not to say something about how we could help. That was another Southern woman thing – to offer help even when the person didn't need, deserve, or ask for it.

"Yes, I hope you are being discreet about this new information you learned. I'd hate to see it in your newsletter or such." She sat silently on the other end of the phone.

"Well, Lois, I have not yet decided what my next newsletter will be, but if Willie gives me permission to talk about her great-grandmother and Bela to talk about her great-grandfather – permission I ask for out of respect not responsibility since these are now public documents – then I may well write about this in the future." I sighed. "Now, if there's not anything else, I have work to do."

My finger was poised over the disconnect button when Lois said, "Please don't, Paisley." Her voice had gone plaintive, all the self-righteousness gone. "You don't understand all that is at risk here."

I looked up and met Mika's eyes. She shook her head; she didn't understand what Lois meant either. A quick glance to Mary and Xzanthia told me they were confused, too. "What do you mean, Lois? What could be at risk? Sharing this information only shines good light on everyone involved."

"Not if you don't think what Martha Johnson did was good," her voice was very quiet. Then, she said, "Never mind. I shouldn't have said anything. Have a good day." She hung up.

For a very long minute, I just stared at the phone on my desk, but when I looked up, everyone else looked as puzzled as I did. "What just happened?"

Mika shook her head. "I have no idea. You certainly sucked the wind from her sails, though. That was wild."

"Yeah, but didn't it sound like she had something else to say? What else could be 'at stake?' All the people involved are dead." She was frowning so hard her eyebrows almost touched.

"True," I said, not sure what else to do or say at that moment.

"Their descendants aren't," Xzanthia said as she sat down.

"What do you mean, Xzanthia?" Mika asked.

Xzanthia shook her head. "I don't know honestly. But I know fear when I hear it, and that woman was scared."

She was right, I suddenly realized. All that bluster. All that anger. It had just been covering up the fact that Lois was terrified. The last thing she said before she hung up was complete fear speaking. "What is she afraid of?" I asked, taking a chair at the table, too. Now that Xzanthia had pointed out that there was more to that call than what was said, all my nerves were on edge. We were missing something.

After a few seconds, Mary sat down, too and held up a finger. "Now, hear me out because this is all just conjecture. But what if Lois had something to do with Dudley Davenport's death?"

I squinted at my friend and tried to see how she had made that leap in thought. It sounded just as absurd as Lois and Bela claiming that obviously Martha Johnson had killed

Azrael Brown because he was gay. I sucked in a deep breath. "That's it."

"Care to share with the class?" Mika asked.

Mary nodded. "Right? That could be it, couldn't it?"

"I think so." I took a deep breath. "What if Lois killed Dudley Davenport for the same reason she and Bela thought Martha Johnson killed Azrael?"

Xzanthia stared from me to Mary and then to Mika. "Give us a minute," she said, gesturing between herself and Mika.

I was dying to explain all the threads that wove together to make that theory feel more and more plausible the longer I thought about it, but I held my tongue.

Xzanthia and Mika stared at each other for a long time, and when they both said, "Oh!" at almost the same second, I started to believe in telepathy.

"She killed him because she didn't want a gay man to adopt a child," Mika finally said. "Whoa."

"Or she didn't want a gay man to adopt a black child," Xzanthia added.

"Or she didn't want a white man to adopt a black child," Mary finished.

I dropped back against my chair. "Are we really thinking this? That this old woman would have killed someone because of her own prejudices?" The minute the sentence left my mouth I realized how naïve I sounded. Of course, people had killed people over their own bigotry for all of human history. Look at Dr. King. Matthew Shepherd. Trayvon Martin. Our ideologies were more valuable than human lives a profoundly terrifying number of times. "Sorry," I said. "That was dumb."

Xzanthia waved a hand. "The question really is do we

have any proof that she did this? If not, then we are leaping to conclusions, just as they did."

I nodded. "Right? We need evidence. Motive is not enough." I paused. "And we don't really even have motive yet, just conjecture."

"Alright," Mary said as she stood and flipped to a new page on the flip chart that still stood in the corner. "How do we get evidence?"

For the next hour, we brainstormed plans for how to get Lois to confess or, at the very least, reveal something really incriminating. We talked about all arriving at her house to pretend and apologize, but that didn't really work because we didn't have anything to apologize for and none of us could lie worth spit.

Mika suggested we simply tell Forest our suspicions and leave him to do the investigating, but the rest of us dismissed that idea because it required Forest to have too much faith in us. And given how sure we were that we were right and how little evidence me we actually had, that would be asking a lot of the deputy.

Finally, we landed on what was actually an honest and reasonable idea. We decided to hold a brunch the next morning at my house and invite all the "stakeholders" as Xzanthia called them to come and talk through the information we'd found about Azrael, Jarvis, and Martha. To discuss how everyone felt about what was uncovered and let everyone speak their piece. On the surface, this would be a reconciliation gathering, and we did want that to happen, too, especially between Willie and Bela since they were land kin and had such strong connections.

But we also hoped we could trip up Lois and get her to admit what we all heartily believed to be true: she had killed Dudley Davenport, and she was afraid if anyone pried too much further into Azrael Brown's death, they'd figure out what she had done.

That theory, however, did bring up something we had all overlooked until Mary pointed it out. "Who did kill Azrael though?"

After we finished the last bits of organizing to do and loaded all the relevant boxes of material, including the two original boxes from the Historical Society collection, we all headed home to think further and get some much-needed downtime.

If had been in my 20s or even my 30s, I might have pushed myself to "get ahead" with research to see if I could figure out who killed Azrael Brown or even to see if I could find a new angle to lure Lois into revealing herself as Davenport's killer. But I'd learned that pushing myself when I was this tired and burnt-out was counterproductive. Finally, I'd accepted the fact that the time I most needed rest was when I felt like I had the least amount of time to do it.

So I went home, made a big bowl of peanut butter popcorn, prepared a plate full of wet paper towels so I could clean my fingers after nibbles, and sat down for a Fillion-thon and my project. For the next six hours, I sat, ate, sewed, and clicked "continue" on the "Are you still watching?" pop-up. Then, I took a melatonin and went to bed.

Then, just like that, I woke up at 6am, rested, and with a totally bonkers theory that I knew, somewhere deep behind my sternum, was right. But because I am a good friend, I waited until 7am to text Mika, Mary, and Xzanthia over and over again until they replied and agreed to come over. With breakfast.

By 7:15, the four of us were gathered in my living room, and I was telling them what *The Rookie* and some wacky dreams that involved cruise ships and donut holes had taught me - that we were going after the wrong woman.

"What in your early Sunday morning mind are you talking about, Paisley Sutton?" Mary asked when I finished my very weaving and long story about my dreams and Nathan and how they'd solved this case with a garage door. Okay, so I understood the confusion since that clip from the show had nothing to do with what I had figured out, but it was so funny that I had to share.

Finally, though, I said. "Lois didn't do it."

Mika and Mary exchanged a look and then stared at me.

Xzanthia, though, she didn't bat an eye. "Nope, Bela did."

Chapter Ten

Since Xzanthia was obviously the smartest and most straightforward of us in the room, I let her explain why she had thought we were focusing on the wrong person.

"First," she said, "I was thinking about the two of you," she said, glancing from Mika to me. "Mika, if Paisley came to you and said she stole a loaf of bread because Sawyer wanted it and she didn't have any money, and now, she was going to be charged with stealing and probably lose custody, what would you do?"

"I'd say I stole it obvi—ooooh," Mika said. "Lois is covering for Bela.

Mary sighed. "She's not scared for herself. She's scared for her friend. That makes sense."

"Exactly," I agreed. "And she made up the whole story about Martha Johnson killing Azrael for the same reason."

"To deflect attention away from Bela when it looked like Forest might be getting close to solving Davenport's murder," Mary finished.

"Yes," Xzanthia said. "But I think there's something more there, too."

This time, I was the one who was flabbergasted. "What do you mean?"

"I think Bela also knows who killed her great-grandfather and didn't want that news coming out either," Xzanthia said as she turned to look at the archival boxes I had set on a side table by the window. She looked at the dates on the end of the boxes and opened one before taking out a single folder. "Remember this letter from Jarvis to Azrael in 1865?"

I stared at the letter that she was now holding up against the folder to face us. "Sorry?"

"Right," she said, "It looks like every other letter. And when I first read it, I thought it was another sweet letter between people who loved each other."

"It's not?" Mika asked.

"No, it is," Xzanthia said just a bit sharply, "but it's also more." She turned the folder back to face her and read, "'Thomas has been to visit me while you've been away. I must say he is quite upset about the current situation and feels that given the impending outcome of the war, we are making poor decisions.'"

"Oh, yeah, I remember that, but I took that as poor farming decisions or maybe something political," I said.

"That's what I had thought, too," Xzanthia said. "But there's another letter, just a couple weeks later when Azrael is still away in Richmond." She slid the first folder back into the box and pulled out the second. "Here, Jarvis says, 'Thomas was by again, and I must ask that you return immediately. His concerns are getting more virulent, and I am not sure I can keep him appeased much longer.'"

"Oh!" Mika chirped.

"Right?!" Xzanthia said. "We thought we were reading that Thomas was upset about farming, but what if he was upset about Jarvis and his father?"

Suddenly, everything clicked into place, and my heart started to pound. "We need to call Forest," I said as I reached for my phone.

"I'd recommend against that," Bela Brown said from my open front door, where she stood with a shotgun, her pick-up's headlights and roof lights shining into the house as if it was being interrogated. "I'd truly prefer that you keep this information to yourself. I value my privacy."

Chapter Eleven

As I stared at Bela Brown in her house coat, fuzzy slippers, full face of make-up, and perfectly coifed hair, I couldn't decide if I wanted to laugh or cry. She looked ridiculous, and she also looked ferociously angry. I opted for fear rather than laughter given that she looked angry enough to shoot without another warning.

Slowly, I put my hand back in my lap and waited until Bela came the rest of the way into the house. "I know you weren't expecting me until about 10, but I found I couldn't wait longer to hear what you had to say." Her voice was the kind of syrupy sweet and southern that TV shows often used to portray people from our part of the US. Little did they know that this particular tone was only used by angry Southern women who had been taught that passive-aggressive was better than outright aggressive.

"Well, we're glad you're here," Xzanthia said flatly. "Please join us. We were just talking about your great-grandaddy Azrael." She deftly slid the folder she'd been holding back into the box just as if it was any other piece of paper that needed to be put away.

Bela barely glanced at it as she took a seat in the rocking chair next to the front door. "And what were you saying?"

"Oh," Mary said, "we were just talking about how good a farmer he was. He not only managed to keep the farm operational during the war years, but he was one of the few planters that ended the war with a fully functioning farm, even after Emancipation."

I swallowed my smile at how seamlessly Mary lied as a good church-going woman. I was also quite impressed at how much she knew about plantation owners at the outcomes of the Civil War. She was right. Many of them went bankrupt or something of the sort after they had to free the people they enslaved.

"That's right," I continued. "Part of what we wanted to talk with you about when you came this morning was that the Historical Society wanted to do an exhibit about your great-grandaddy Azrael. Show off some of his most important papers, maybe include images of his house, and, if you would, have you speak about his legacy. What do you think?"

The shotgun lowered just a bit in Bela's arms, and she smiled. "Well, that would be right nice. I have one of his old suits, too, if you'd like it." She turned to Xzanthia. "You could keep it protected, right?"

"Oh yes, we have a plexiglass case just for clothing that we put on display. It would look lovely there." She cleared her throat and began to list off a variety of the documents that she thought would factor well into the extremely flattering exhibit about Azrael Brown, and while she rambled on, I caught Mika's eye and touched my wrist.

She frowned before looking down at her own wrist,

where she wore her smartwatch. The watch that could text for help. Immediately, she slid her other hand over her wrist, and then I could just barely see that she was gripping the watch to send its automated emergency alert. Forest would get the message within seconds and be on his way.

Unfortunately, I also got the message since I was one of Mika's emergency contacts, and my phone started to vibrate loudly on the table beside me.

"Leave it," Bela said as I turned to look and see what the screen said. Fortunately, the name on the screen was Mik, and while anyone who knew us well knew that's what I called my best friend, I had to hope that Bela either didn't know that or couldn't read the name from a few feet away. I turned my head back to face her, hoping that the phone would stop buzzing and be forgotten.

Fortunately, Mary and Xzanthia were on a roll with their discussion of this fake exhibit. Mary said, "We talked with Willie, and she and her family would like to host the opening reception at your great-grandfather's house with you as the mistress of ceremonies." Mary swallowed and then continued, "She said she wanted to pay tribute to your great-grandfather for his kindness to her great-grandmother."

I clenched my jaw at the power it must have taken Mary to tell that whopper of a lie, but it seemed to work because Bela actually set the shotgun across her legs and sat back a little. "Do you have ideas about what food you'd serve?" she asked, clearly getting wrapped up in the idea of something to honor her family.

The four of us listed off the highest end hors d'oeuvres we could think of. Everything from caviar to lobster to deviled eggs. We were pulling out all the fantastical stops for this party we would most definitely not be throwing, either because we were dead or Bela was in jail. Hopefully the latter.

Bela had just begun to detail the décor scheme she'd prefer when a police siren sounded from just up the road. She immediately lifted that shotgun and pointed it right at me. "I'm sorry to do this, Paisley, but I need you to come here."

Every instinct in my body told me that if I got close to her I was a dead woman, but when she clicked off the safety, I decided I better move. I was taking my first step toward her when a large arm reached over and slammed down on Bela's arms, forcing the gun to the ground. Then, that arm was around the tiny woman, holding her tight.

"Uncle Saul," Mika said with a wail. "You got the message."

"You call, baby girl, I'm coming," he said as he restrained Bela with ease. "Now what exactly is going on here?"

Moments later, Forest rushed in and quickly arrested Bela Brown for threatening us. Then, while she sat outside in his car with the air conditioning running because he wasn't cruel and it was already almost 90 degrees outside, we gave him our statements and then told him about what we believed we had pieced together about both Azrael's and Davenport's deaths.

"So she killed Dudley because he was gay?" he asked.

"I don't know. Maybe," Mika said. "Or maybe she was mad that her great-granddaddy Thomas hadn't inherited the property and Dudley had bought it. Or maybe because Dudley was adopting a young black woman. Or . . ."

"We hope you will be able to get more answers," Xzanthia said. "I will give you anything you need in terms of documents."

"Thank you," Forest said. "All of you. Now, your husband is on his way, so I suggest you relax until he gets here."

"You called him?" I said with a mixture of relief and frustration.

"Paisley, when a 911 call comes from the sheriff's house and you work for the sheriff, you call," he said and then walked out the door to go book his suspect.

"I can't say I blame him," Mary said. "I would have called, too."

I couldn't really say I blamed him either.

By the time Lois, Willie, and William arrived as planned at 10am, Bela had officially been charged with Dudley Davenport's murder. Forest had texted to let me know and told me that he'd matched Bela's fingerprint to one he lifted from the scrap of plastic found in the pumphouse. When he confronted her with that bit of evidence, she confessed. So Davenport's murder was solved.

So we were able to tell the Abramses that the murder case was closed and also give Lois a space to explain why she had been so hostile the night before. Unfortunately, she apologized with all the sincerity of Sawyer when he's angry with me, but Willie and William were gracious and kind, despite her continued hostility.

Before she left, I asked her whether Bela had confessed to her. "Is that why you protected her?"

Lois snarled, "No, Bela is smart. She didn't tell anyone. Not even when I asked her why she had a dolly on her front porch. She made up some story about moving a heavy garden pot. But the next morning I heard the news about that man's body, and I knew."

I sighed. "You saw a hand truck and that was the only clue you needed?"

"No, I knew that Bela's great-grandfather Thomas had killed his dad because he was a f— "

"Absolutely not," I said before she could finish that word. "No, that word is not allowed in my house."

After a startled glare at me, she went on. "Bela had always felt that her great-grandfather had done the right thing because his dad had dishonored his mother with that other man. And she was right. Those people have no respect for the institution of marriage."

Mika scoffed and walked out of the living room, but her disgust didn't slow Lois down at all.

"And when that, em, gay man and his lover moved into Bela's family home," she sneered in the Abramses' direction, "I spent weeks talking her out of burning it down and promised to help her get it back."

"How did the house go out of the family anyway?" Mary asked. "Didn't Thomas leave it to his children?"

"No, after the War of Northern Aggression ended," Lois said, "the Browns lost everything. That Emancipation Proclamation ruined them. They had to sell the house, and Bela's family could only keep that little piece of land that her house was on. They were robbed."

"And Bela couldn't afford to buy it when it got put up for public auction," Xzanthia said. "I can understand how sad that might make someone."

"It didn't make her sad," Lois spat. "It made her furious, and rightly so. It was *her* house, and all these people got to live in it when she just had that little shed. It wasn't fair."

"You want to talk about fair—" I started, but Xzanthia

laid a hand on my arm and shook her head. "Well, I think you'll be able to see Bela tomorrow. I'm sure she'd appreciate a friendly visit," I said through gritted teeth. "Now, if you'll excuse us, I'd rather not have you and your hatefulness in my house any longer. You can see yourself out."

Most of my dad's family would have been appalled at what he would have seen as my rudeness, but I was done trying to be civil to people whose attitudes and actions kept people hurt people I love.

Lois didn't say a word. Just stood and walked out the door, slamming it so hard behind her that the glass rattled.

"Whoa," Willie said after the reverberations from Lois' visit had ebbed. "It is going to take me a long time to process all of this. But thank you all."

"Yes, thank you," William said. "We will be sure to honor Dudley Davenport in the house. In his own way, it sounds like he was trying to make a refuge for people there."

Xzanthia nodded. "And I actually have some more news. Last night, I called in a favor with a friend I have in a certain government agency. He was able to locate Elizabeth Russell, now Elizabeth Jacobs. She lives in Washington, DC and runs a children's theater now."

"You found her?" I said as tears clogged my throat. "Wow."

"I've sent her an email, and if she gets back in touch, I'll let you know. I hope to be able to talk to her and tell her what we've learned about her adopted father's death," Xzanthia said.

"You'll keep us posted about if she gets back in touch?" Willie asked.

"I will," Xzanthia said.

For a few more minutes, we sat together, mostly in

silence, and then everyone slowly headed home, the fright of Bela's gunpoint arrival and the weight of all that Lois had said had drained everyone. We needed time to rest.

Santi and Sawyer were home by noon, and once they both saw I was fine and got an update – slightly tamed for Sawyer – they were all news about the fish they'd caught and the bear they'd seen and the number of packets of ramen they'd made over the campfire. It was a quiet afternoon and evening as we unpacked all their gear and washed everything to rid it of the smell of campfire.

By 7pm, we were all in bed with our books and our warm blankets, and while I didn't check to see, I think all of us were sound asleep by 8. It had been a big week.

And it wasn't slowing down with the start of the next one. Before we even got Sawyer off to camp for the day, Santi and I had both gotten calls about the case. Forest told Santi that Bela Brown was making claims of assault and grand larceny against the Abramses and that they'd found a stash of formaldehyde in Bela's back shed, where an uncle had apparently had a taxidermy shop at one point. "Apparently, she'd learned some basic techniques when working with him as a child," Santi told me when he hung up. "Knew, at least, how to keep the smell down."

"Well, that answers a few questions, but why didn't she just bury him?" I asked.

Santi tilted his head. "Do you remember how long it took you to dig that hole to plant the hydrangea out front?"

I sighed. "Now that you mention it, embalming does sound easier." I shook my head. "At least physically.

As soon as Santi was out the door, my phone rang. It

was Xzanthia asking me to come to the historical society because Elizabeth Jacobs was on her way from DC.

Thus, our morning was frantic, but Sawyer went off to camp with excitement for a day of swimming, playing basketball, and making some kind of craft. And I even had a second to drink a cup of coffee.

Xzanthia had already begun to organize our presentation to Elizabeth, which was good because I really had no idea what we were going to say to a woman who had not actually ever been adopted by a man who was murdered because someone else hated how he loved. My friend, however, she did know.

She'd put together a slideshow of images of Dudley and James, images she'd culled from old social media accounts and the few newspaper articles she'd found about either of them. Then, she'd created an album, with the Abramses' permission, of images of the house as it was when they bought it. It would have been nice to have pictures from when it was furnished and lived in, but at least this gave Elizabeth a chance to see what might have been her home, if she wanted to.

"Xzanthia," I said after flipping through the small photo album, "what if this is all too much for her? What if she doesn't want to know all of this?"

"Then, we won't show her. The decision is completely hers, but it's my job to present the story as fully as I can. That's always my job. How people read that story? If they do? That's not mine to worry about."

Her words tapped this tiny ball of tension that I'd carried ever since that UDC meeting, and the ball disintegrated. I didn't have to worry about how what I learned was received. I only had to share it. What a freeing place to be.

"Okay," I said with far more enthusiasm. "What can I do?"

"I want her to feel welcome, so could you get us some sandwiches and drinks for lunch?" she said as she continued to arrange her notes and then pull files for the table-top display she wanted to have ready for Elizabeth.

"Absolutely. Just the three of us? We're not having a gathering?" I wasn't sure what I wanted her answer to be. Part of me really wanted everyone who had participated in this wild week of discovery to meet this young woman who had been at the center of it all, but I also thought that maybe we would be too much, too many people touching her story.

"Yes, just the three of us. I told our guest that if she wanted to meet the people who had helped or see Davenport's home, we could make that happen later today or another time. But for now, it's just the three of us."

I headed up to the deli at the grocery store and got a small platter of various sandwiches, a few bags of chips in different flavors, and several bottled drinks. The leftovers would find a good home, but I wanted to give everyone options.

When I returned from the store, Xzanthia was ready to do a run-through of her presentation. "An audience of one is still an audience," she told me, and while I knew she was being professional, I also realized that this particular audience was very special to both of us.

As usual, the director was poised and clear, walking through everything she had prepared with just the right amount of historical context to let the audience form their own opinions about the situations surrounding the specifics she was discussing. So when she introduced me as part of the presentation, I was surprised. "You want me to talk?"

Xzanthia nodded. "But not now. You're at your best when you speak extemporaneously and from the heart. But yes, I'd like you to tell Elizabeth what it meant for you to learn about Dudley and James and what they will continue to mean for you in the future." She studied my face. "Can you do that?"

"Yes," I said quietly.

"Can you do that without crying?"

"Absolutely not," I said. "That's the 'from the heart' bit you like so much."

We both laughed, and then, we spent the rest of the morning typing in the transcriptions that the UDC volunteers had made. These women were very good at this work, so good that while I wasn't sure how she'd do it, I knew Xzanthia would be recruiting them as volunteers for the society.

Just before noon, someone knocked on the front door of the Society, and Xzanthia opened the door to a beautiful, tall black woman in her 20s. The woman wore long braids and a flowing blouse over jeans, and when she smiled at first Xzanthia and then me, I felt this strong sense of recognition. "Have we met before?" I asked as I shook Elizabeth's hands.

She shook her head. "I don't think so," she said with a smile. "But it's nice to meet you now."

"Likewise," I said. "A true honor."

A pink tinge came to Elizabeth's cheeks, and she smiled again. "Thank you for inviting me."

Xzanthia led us back into the research room and asked Elizabeth if she'd like some lunch, which the strict director had agreed could be set up at one end of the table, far from the materials, so that we wouldn't have to move around during our time together.

"Oh yes, please," Elizabeth said. "I forgot that the last stretch of the drive from Culpeper to Octonia is a bit barren of stopping places."

I smiled. "You can say that again. Heaven forbid you have to pee during those miles."

"Exactly," Elizabeth said as she helped herself to a couple of sandwich quarters and a Cheerwine.

We ate and chatted about Elizabeth's theater and their recent production of *Taming of the Shrew*, which she had set in a 1960s small town, using the Jim Crow policies of the time to create the divisions rather than class.

As she talked, a chill settled over me as she told us about how she had cast Kate as a black maid in a white household. The historical reverberations of what we'd been looking at with Martha Johnson sounded like gongs in my spirit. I shouldn't have been surprised at what the ancestors could do, but still, I found myself almost speechless with the resonance.

Finally, though, Xzanthia began her talk, and Elizabeth asked to see everything. "I didn't get to live this life, but the hope and affection that Dudley gave me, it carried me even so."

"How did you guys meet?" I asked, hoping that Xzanthia wouldn't mind my interruption.

"He and James saw me in a production at the Four County Players and came up to introduce themselves after the show. We stayed in touch, and eventually, they found out

I lived in foster care. That's when they decided to adopt me."

She took a deep breath. "But then James got sick, and while Dudley continued to invite me over and come to every one of my shows, he couldn't manage the adoption process and caring for his husband. I understood, mostly."

Xzanthia looked at me. "Oh, Elizabeth, that's not why he didn't adopt you that first time. Their application to adopt was denied by the county."

"What?" she said, leaning forward. "Why?"

We gave her a minute, and then she let out a long slow breath. "Because they were gay. Of course." She wiped a tear from her eye.

"But then, once the climate was more accepting, he applied again," Xzanthia continued, "when you were about 14, we think."

"He did?" Elizabeth said. "I didn't know that."

"Oh yes," Xzanthia said and handed her a copy of the second adoption application. "And he was approved."

Tears streamed down Elizabeth's face. "He was going to do it by himself?" She kept staring at the paper.

"He was, but he was killed before he could," Xzanthia said.

"Excuse me. Did you say he was killed?" Elizabeth's face had drained of blood.

I nodded. "He was. Strangled by a woman who didn't want him to be able to adopt you."

"Allegedly," Xzanthia said. "She's been charged but not convicted."

Elizabeth closed her eyes and shook her head. "Wow." She tilted her head toward the ceiling, eyes still closed. "I'm going to need a minute with that one."

"Take your time," Xzanthia said. "We can do this at any pace that works for you."

A few moments later, Elizabeth opened her eyes and looked at Xzanthia. "So he didn't just leave town? Leave me?"

All the tears I had been holding back poured out of my eyes now, and I was up and out of my seat before I could think. I knelt down beside Elizabeth's chair and said, "No, honey. He didn't. He was going to make you his family officially. He wanted you."

Xzanthia took the chair on the other side of Elizabeth, and quietly, the three of us cried for what this young woman had lost.

Then, for the next hour, Xzanthia showed her everything she had compiled about her father, as Elizabeth insisted on calling him – had always called him, even after she thought he abandoned her – and his life. Elizabeth asked lots of questions, and those we couldn't answer we wrote down so we could find those answers for her.

But when Xzanthia handed her the photo album of Dudley's house, Elizabeth flipped through it and then said, "Could I see it in person? It's been so long."

I was already typing a text to Willie before she finished speaking. Willie's enthusiastic invitation was almost instantaneous. "The owners are so excited to meet you. We can go now."

Within 15 minutes, the three of us were walking up the steps to the Abramses' house and crying again, as Willie, her own face wet with tears, met Elizabeth with a hug on the steps. "Welcome home," she said.

Elizabeth sniffled and smiled, but when William stepped forward, she stopped cold.

William slowed his approach and put out his hand. "I'm William, Willie's husband. It's nice to meet you."

Slowly, she reached out and shook his hand. "I'm sorry, but you look just like photos I've seen of my birth father, Winston."

William froze in place. "Winston?"

I stepped up and put my arm around Elizabeth's shoulders.

"Yes, Winston Abrams. He's my birth father."

William then crumped under a sob and sank to the porch floor.

All of us stood, stunned, at the overwhelming emotion that had taken over this huge man's body. I looked to Willie as she put her hand on her husband's shoulder before looking at Elizabeth.

"Winston was William's brother." She choked back her own tears. "This is your uncle."

Slaying at Stanway: Chapter One

I've always dreamed of inheriting a grand old house since I was 7 years old, after reading a novel about a young woman who got such a thing. I imagined a sprawling house with comfortable rooms and lots of space, both inside and out, for roaming. Space was what I craved most.

Growing up in a small cottage in a university town with my two parents, three dogs, five cats, and a parakeet, I always longed for more space, especially when my mother set up the stray cat rescue out of our front, screened-in porch.

Critters were always everywhere – in my bed, in the kitchen, sometimes even sleeping in the shower. I loved them all and had sweet nicknames for each of them. But sometimes, I just wanted to not have to take care of anyone but myself.

When things had gotten too hectic with fur and fangs inside the house, I would go outside. I started by simply tidying up the neglected flower beds in front of the ranch house my parents had bought when they were first married.

Even at 7, I knew that most of the green plants growing under the azalea hedge were weeds. So most afternoons after school, I'd tuck myself into the growing shade of the shrubs and pull-out ground ivy and clover and even wire grass.

Then, as I got the yard into good stead, I started asking my parents for money to buy flowers. With my few dollars in hand, I'd ride my bike to the hardware store on the Square and pick up four packs of whatever they had, usually pansies, petunias, or impatiens. I'd plant them in front of the azaleas.

By the time I was a teenager, the lawn in my parents' front yard had gradually been removed, and I had replaced it with an elaborate and tidy cottage garden with weaving paths, a bench for seating, and even a small arbor that bridged the walkway from the mailbox to the front door. Everyone in the neighborhood loved my design, but no one wanted to do what I had done. I knew because I had tried to convince them to give it a go. But the most they ever did was add some petunias to the bed by their mailboxes.

Eventually, I realized that my interest in flowers and landscaping was unique and that most people didn't have the time or didn't want to put the effort into maintaining anything but grass. However, everyone loved flowers, and when I found that I could enhance my parents' yard with lilies and irises, even an English rose bush, I started my first business, selling cut flowers to my neighbors.

When it came time for me to go to college, I went off to North Carolina to study horticulture at NC State, and when I came back to Virginia, I started working as a greenhouse supervisor for a local garden center, a center I was managing the day my world upended.

If you'd asked me six months ago what I thought my life

would look like 180 days later, I would have told you that I was looking forward to harvesting zinnias and making tabletop arrangements to sell at the garden center. I might have said I hoped to be able to add that money to my savings and maybe, if all went well, be able to buy a little craftsman cottage in the mountainside town of Crozet in a year or two.

I would not have told you that my parents would be killed in a tragic car crash one summer night when their car hydroplaned off a mountainside. I wouldn't have told you that I would, as their only child, inherit everything they owned, including the ranch house with the neglected front garden and the dozen stray cats on the porch. I wouldn't have said that I would soon discover, when going through my mother's papers, that I actually owned a house in the English Cotswolds, a house recently inherited from my aunt and the woman after whom I was named. I wouldn't have said that my entire life would be entirely different. I wouldn't have said that at all.

And yet, here I am, a woman in my early 40s, never married with no children, about to set off into an entirely new life in an entirely new country. I've lived one of those lives that often seemed so ordinary as to not be worth noticing, at least to myself. I've done all the usual professional things – college, of course, and my job at the garden center. I have friends, good friends from college, women I talk to often via text and see maybe once a year. I've become friends with some of the folks from work, too, and on a weekend, I usually go out with them to see a movie or get dinner, sometimes take in a concert or play. But no one in my life is my person per se. No best friend. No husband.

I was a bit lonely but not because I didn't have friends. No, I was lonely because I didn't have that special person to talk about my day with, someone whose hobbies I could learn to understand and maybe enjoy myself. Someone to cuddle up to on cold nights. But after a decade or so of on and off online dating, I'd given up and decided that the man of my dreams was just going to have to find me. I was done trying to find him. "It's my power position," I told my college roommate on the phone one night. "I'm not exactly trying to manifest him because I don't really even know what that means. But I'm trusting that if I live my life on my terms, he'll find me."

My old roommate had been more than a bit skeptical, pointing out that no one was going to break into my house, in all likelihood, to date me. I admitted she had a point but also reiterated that I was so weary of online dating. "Short of finding a matchmaker, he may have to," I'd said. "I just cannot do online dating anymore. It's too demoralizing."

I had really tried at online dating. I'd done the flirty thing, the question thing, even the first date thing itself. And while I'd met some nice people, I found I was spending an inordinate amount of time trying to pry interest out of men – "Hi. You're cute," seemed to be a pretty standard response to my "Hi," and I didn't really know where to go with that – or to deflect the inappropriate photos or commentary that came into my inbox. As I figured it, I was about 1 for 20 in finding men I might actually want to date and that was after whittling out all the guys with no profile pic, who posed with a fish, or who shared absolutely no information about themselves in their profiles. At this point, I was more likely to hit it off with a burglar than any of the men on the dating sites.

Thus, when I found myself more or less family-less, without any good friends nearby, and without any prospects on the dating scene, I decided to take my new property inheritance in England as a sign and go there. I had nothing to lose by moving to my mother's hometown and doing what I'd started doing back when I was a teenager – running a flower farm.

It was relatively easy to get the business set-up, even from Virginia, so while I had a lawyer at my disposal for the execution of my parents' wills, I asked him to do the necessaries, using my new address, to create my flower farm and be sure I could get work as soon as I arrived.

Then, I checked in with the lawyer of record for my great aunt's property to be sure I could access it when I arrived, booked airline tickets, and gave notice at my job. All that was left was to end my lease, arrange an estate sale for my parents' belongings, and rehome the dozens of plants I had babied for years. The plant placement was by far the most difficult part of the process since, of course, I had to be sure they would go to good homes. It wasn't just anyone who could care properly for a banana tree, after all.

I was not delusional. I knew I'd need to grieve sometime, but with all the arrangements for the move and such, I didn't give myself time to do so. The loss was too great to deal with immediately, I told my friends. I needed time to let it sink in, to come to terms with the fact that I was, with the exception of a few cousins I had met once or twice, alone in the world. That realization was too much for me to carry in the midst of what had to be done, so I tucked it away and plowed ahead. To England.

Thus, three months after my parents' death, I was on the way "across the pond" to begin life anew and, I knew, to grieve. As hard as that was. And it was very, very hard.

When I stepped off the bus, er, coach in Stow-on-the-Wold, the first thing I saw was the town square with its small monument that reminded me, probably quite intentionally, of the much larger-scale one I had just walked around at Piccadilly Circus in London. In an attempt to ease my transition, I'd taken a layover in the city to take in the National Museum and a few shows. Surprisingly, it had been *Back to the Future: The Musical* that I had loved best. Maybe it was homesickness.

My new life now before me, I brushed my long dark hair off my neck, straightened my calf-length puffer jacket, and strode into town, my suitcase splashing mud against my jeans and booties. I hoped my aunt's house had a washer and dryer.

Still, now that I was in my new town, I was eager to make it my own and immediately asked directions to Nigella Smith's home at the local pub, The Pig and Cane. The woman behind the bar had turned to the man cooking fries in the back kitchen, and they had talked for a few minutes as they tried to parse out which Nigella Smith this middle-aged American woman with the huge suitcase might be looking for.

"Reckon it's the one with the leg thing?" the barkeep asked.

"Nah, she hasn't gone by Smith since she married that Scottish fella. Could be the one down the lane with the sheep?" the cook said.

The barkeep seemed to consider this option and then shook his head. "Nah, she's a Sutton now." She turned back to me.

"We need a bit more information if you please. Why are you looking for her?"

I might have been put off by this question if but for two

things. I was an American and, therefore, used to personal questions asked by strangers, and I had just watched these people try to help me and felt the least I could do was give them a bit more to go on. "She was my great-aunt. She died just a couple of months ago. Does that help?"

"Oh yes," the barkeep said. "You'll be meaning Auntie Jelly then, won't she, Mick?"

The cook nodded. "God rest her soul."

"Thank you," I said. "Could you point me to where she lived?" I felt a bit abrupt repeating my inquiry to people who had, apparently, known my aunt well enough to call her Jelly, but I was exhausted and just wanted to put down my suitcase and put up my feet.

"Definitely, but let me take you up there. It's a fair piece, and with that suitcase, it'll take you far longer than you'd like, I expect," the cook said as he hung his apron on a hook by the door to the kitchen. "Be back in twenty, Margaret," he said as he hefted my suitcase and led me out the door.

It turned out that the cook was named Michael "Mick" Harper, and his family had lived in Stow for, as he put it, "near on 1000 years."

I had expressed my awe and slight disbelief at that fact, but when Mick pointed out that the town had been founded, by most accounts, in the 1100s, I reminded myself that America was just a baby country in comparison. Mick went on to explain, with a jovial lift to his voice, that the first residents here were monks but that "my people were definitely not of the cloth unless you count wool."

I was charmed by this very English and apparently VERY local man, and I grew more so as he talked about his wife and kids, about how the children were obsessed with rugby at the moment and so he never knew who would have what bruise when he got home, and about how he hoped I'd come into the pub from time to time to relax and catch up. He said "catch up" as if we'd known each other for decades. I liked that.

"You been here before?" he asked. "You know, to visit your aunt."

I smiled at the memory. "Once," I said, "when I was seven. We came for a few days, but all I can remember is a tire swing and an old lady with boots."

"That'd be Aunt Jelly then," he said. "And that tire swing is famous round these parts. All of the neighbor kids played on it. Now that I have kids of my own, I realize that was Jelly's way of giving the parents, especially the mums, a little break. Sort of like the neighborhood granny, I guess."

The image of my aunt as the neighborhood grandmother gave me a ping of joy. "Maybe that's why she left me the house then?" I mused aloud. "Maybe she remembered me swinging on that swing?"

"Aye, I'm sure she did," Mick said. "She had a memory like a steel trap." Mick glanced over at me out of the corner of his eye. "Forgive me asking, Miss, but do you have a family who'll be joining you?"

My throat tightened just a bit. "No, it's just me." I took a deep breath. "But maybe I'll invite all the neighborhood kids over to swing." I smiled over at my driver. "Maybe save your loves from getting a few bruises."

Mick laughed, and by the time he pulled his ancient Mini Cooper up at the door of a lanky farmhouse that seemed to spread, like a kid making a snow-angel, across the gravel courtyard, I knew I had made my first friend. "You come on down to the pub anytime you need anything," he told me as he pulled m suitcase out of the trunk, something he called a "boot." "Me and Margaret are always happy to help our neighbors."

I smiled. "Thank you, and forgive me asking. Is Margaret your wife?"

Mick's face went a bright shade of red under his dark hair. "Oh, no ma'am. She's my sister."

A flush to match Mick's spread over my body, but I smiled and said, "It was nice to meet you both. Thank you so much." I held out what I thought was a respectable tip – a five-pound note – to the young man, but he looked at it and turned away.

When he put out a hand and waved through the open car window as he pulled away, I decided I was going to like Stow.

———

My opinion faltered a bit, however, when I unlocked the heavy iron lock on the front door of my aunt's cottage. It was colder inside than it was out, which was saying something because the damp air had already chilled me to the bone and was starting to drift with flakes of snow. Inside, though, the air was even more damp, and from what I could see, there wasn't a heating vent or even a radiator in sight.

Fortunately, I had long ago learned how to build a fire in a fireplace, a skill my father had insisted I perfect just in case the power went out. So after testing the chimney to be sure it drafted, I had a warm fire glowing in the hearth of what was the most delightfully old-fashioned kitchen I had ever seen, never mind the chill and damp. In the center of the room was a long farm table, gouged and scraped by what I thought must have been decades of wear. A long counter spanned one side, and on it, I found a deep farm sink with built-in dish rack and what people would now call a pot-filler faucet but was, I knew from a quick search on the internet, just a practical set up in farmhouse kitchens. As the article said, "One never knew when one might need to rinse a bucket or bathe a chicken."

The walls were a yellow-beige plaster that mimicked the color of the stone that the coach driver had told me was the true marker of the Cotswold architecture, and in one corner, I found a short refrigerator that looked like it was vintage but turned out to be brand-spanking new with a classic look. A little further investigation found that there was a modern dishwasher, a double oven, and even a microwave tucked discretely behind a cabinet door. Aunt Jelly had clearly appreciated old-warm charm *and* new-world amenities, and I really loved the combination too.

The fire going steadily and the kettle by the sink warming water for what I hoped would be a fine English tea soon, I made my way through the rest of the house, crossing the hall into what was clearly a living room with another fireplace, two arm chairs, a table with a half-finished jigsaw puzzle by the window, and a comfy couch facing a small flat-screen TV at the far-end of the room. Further down the hall, I discovered what must have been my aunt's office with a desk, bookshelves, and three filing cabinets, and just beyond that, a half-bath with, again, old-looking but clearly new fixtures.

After lugging my suitcase up a solid set of wooden stairs that ran half the length of the central hallway, I found four bedrooms, all decorated with four-posted beds, antique dressers, and lamps that sat on wooden nightstands. Here, I saw radiators tucked beneath the windows and gave a sigh of relief. Each room also had a fireplace, but I didn't relish making up quite that many fires every day.

At the back of the house, off one of the bedrooms, I located a full bath complete with a steam shower, a soaking tub, and a view out over the Cotswold country-side that left me practically breathless. I could see the rolling pastures for miles around, and the piled-stone walls gave the landscape a gentle gridded pattern that somehow combined both the natural world with a very human one in a way that felt both just and sound.

I decided this view was going to be mine every day and slung my suitcase up on the bed before going down to make that cup of tea to carry with me on the rest of my tour. As I passed back up the hallway, I saw there was another full bathroom, not quite as well appointed as my own but very lovely, in the middle of the hall and was grateful that my guests, should I have any, would have their own space and leave me to mine.

After figuring out how to use a tea diffuser to steep a cup of Earl Gray and adding three teaspoons of sugar to make up for the lack of milk, I made my way back out into the courtyard in front of the house, curious to see what the splaying limbs of the building contained since they didn't seem accessible from the living quarters proper.

Sure enough, as soon as I turned a corner, I found a low-flung building made from the same stone as the house on three walls but open but for a massive wooden timber in the middle on the fourth. The space was full of clean hay, and at one side, I saw an actual manger like the kind Jesus always laid in at the living nativity things at Christmas. Beside it, a black basin full of water stood clear and seemingly cool in the chilly air. "A stable?" I said to myself.

"Yes, ma'am," a man's voice said from just behind me. "This is where Bramble, Clover, and Thistle spend their evenings."

I turned, fully startled, and stared at the rugged, handsome man holding a pitchfork behind me.

"You must be Ms. Hunt," he said. "Sorry to give you a fright. I'm Graham Whitfield, but most folks call me Gray." He started to put out his hand, but when I stared a second too long at the dirt encasing his fingers like gloves, he withdrew it, a slight blush rising to his cheeks.

"Nice to meet you, Gray," I said. "Please call me Nell." I shook off my hesitation and extended my own hand, which he shook firmly without pause. "So I have, what, horses?"

Gray beamed. "No, missus. Miniature donkeys. Want me to show you?"

A kick of delight rose in my chest at the idea of donkeys of any size but especially small ones. "Yes, please."

"Follow me, just watch your step. With the snow, it's a bit mucky back here."

I kept my eyes on the ground as I made my way past what looked to be a sturdy, busy chicken coop that flanked off behind the house, a large patch of freshly turned earth that I took to be a vegetable garden, and out to a wide pasture where I saw three very small animals with very large ears. As soon as the donkeys caught sight of us humans, they began to trot over, braying all the time, and I decided that the sound of a donkey braying was my new favorite sound.

"This one here with the white spot on his nose is Bramble. This girl here is Thistle, and this feisty one is Clover. She'll take to you soon enough, but until then, don't get behind her."

"Because she'll poop on me?" I said with a raised eyebrow.

"Well, that too. But she's a kicker, that one," Gray said as he scratched Thistle's nose. "Feed her some apples though, and she'll soon become your best guardian."

"Guardian?" I asked, confused about what exactly that

meant. Was it some English country term that I didn't know? Maybe some old-world legend about protecting the house or something?

"Oh yes, these donkeys guard the chickens. Most days the birds are out here with them, but because of the snow, I kept them in today. The donkeys keep the hawks and other predators out of the pasture." He reached over and rubbed Clover's head. "Haven't lost a bird yet."

"Well, good job guys," I said as I patted first Thistle, then Bramble, before letting Clover sniff my hand, which I pulled back just in time to avoid getting a nip on the finger. "Oh, she is feisty."

"Told you," Gray said. "But you don't need to worry about them, Missus. I've got it all under control."

"Oh, well thank you, Gray," I paused and looked around. "Forgive me. I'm still figuring things out. Do you work here?"

"Oh yes, ma'am, I'm your farmhand. Been working for Aunt Jelly for going on 15 years now. Took over my chores when the farm work got to be too much for her." He smiled and waved at the patch of turned ground behind her. "She kept herself busy in that garden until the day she died though. Said weeding made her feel calm."

I felt the same way about the work of gardening and let a wave of loss and warmth spread through me as I realized that I and my great aunt shared that love. "Well, the place looks wonderful, and I can tell the animals are well cared for." I paused. "But I'm afraid I can't afford to pay you. I'm just getting set up, and my budget doesn't account for a farmhand, I'm afraid."

Gray nodded. "You don't need to worry about that either, Missus. As I understand it, Aunt Jelly took care of having my salary taken care of, that is if you want to keep me on."

"Oh, well, then, great," I said, not sure how I actually felt about having an employee right away but very certain I wasn't going to fire this man, at least not immediately, if he could help me make this transition. The animals were a delightful addition to my expectations for the place, but I didn't know anything at all about caring for chickens or miniature donkeys. "Maybe you can teach me some of what you do. I'd like to help."

"Of course," he said. "But you get yourself settled first. Then, we'll make you a farmer proper."

"Graham, um, Gray, can I ask you a question?"

"Of course, Missus," he said.

"Did my aunt tell you why she left this place to me?"

Gray studied me a long moment. "You don't know?"

I shook my head. "None of the paperwork was personal, and my aunt didn't leave a letter or anything. I only met her once when I was a kid, so I have no idea why I was her heir."

With one grimy hand, Gray rubbed his chin. "Well, as I understand it . . ." he paused and stared at his feet, "well, missus, I don't know quite how to say this, but she thought you might enjoy the garden." He looked up at me sheepishly.

"Really?" I said. "That's why she gave me this entire house and land, because she thought I'd want the garden. Wow."

Gray looked at me carefully. "That's what she said, missus, was I wrong?"

"Oh no, no. Not at all." I smiled and scanned the property again. "I love to garden. I've always loved it. I just didn't know my great-aunt knew that about me."

"Definitely did," Gray said. "She even said something about your wanting to have a flower farm."

At this, tears sprang to my eyes. "She knew that, too."

Gray nodded.

My mother must have told her sister about my dream. Just the fact that my mom had cared enough to share that information with someone made the grief that I had been holding so carefully at bay threaten to break over my carefully constructed walls. I needed to change the subject.

I turned and studied the garden patch again. "Did, er, Aunt Jelly grow vegetables here?" I asked.

"A few, yes. Some lettuces, rhubarb, and strawberries," he gestured to an unturned patch of brown-green leaves at the far corner of the garden. "But mostly she did flowers. Dahlias and sunflowers, lilies, and irises. Her pride and joy, they were."

Tears sprung afresh to my eyes. "She had a flower garden?" My throat grew tight. "For her own pleasure?"

"Mostly, yeah, but she also did arrangements for weddings and such. Nothing big or fancy, but people loved her flowers." Gray stared affectionately at the garden. "I'd be happy to help you keep up a garden like hers if you'd like, Missus."

"Please, do call me, Nell, and yes, I'd like your help very much." I glanced down at the near empty mug of tea in my hand. "In fact, if you have a minute, I'd like to tell you about my plans, see what you think."

"Your plans, ma'am?"

"Oh yes, as my aunt told you, I'm hoping to open a flower farm here, selling cut flowers and doing arrangements for weddings and such." I stared at the garden patch. "We might need a bit more space, though." I looked over at

Gray hesitantly, afraid that maybe he would find my eagerness to alter my aunt's space rude or invasive.

But he was grinning from ear to ear. "Aunt Jelly is probably dancing a jig right now at that idea." He leaned his pitchfork up against the pasture fence. "Let's get planning."

Gray was a wealth of information about not only the growing conditions for flowers here in the Cotswolds but also what the traditional flowers for funerals, weddings, and other celebrations were. I had known the region was known for remarkable flowers, particularly through the nearby Cheltenham flower show, but I had no sense of what people might expect in the arrangements they might order.

He'd also suggested that I might consider a flower CSA so that I could have a steady income even when events were fewer, like in the winter.

"I like the idea of having a subscription for flowers, but what could I possibly have for subscribers in the cold months?" I asked him as I made notes about options for price points and flowers each month.

Gray sat and thrummed his fingers on the table for a long minute, and then said, "Well, what if you did some seed pod bunches for November, packaged so that people could place them out as food for the birds."

I loved that idea and told him so. "I could even save up my own lard and make suet batches to give them."

"Aye," Gray said. "And then how about swags of yew and boxwood with some berries?"

"Do we have yews and boxwoods here?" I couldn't recall seeing any on the parts of the property I had visited as of yet.

"Not many," Gray said and then waggled his eyebrows, "but loads of people in the area do, and if we asked them to prune just before December, you could help them out by taking away the clippings for your own use."

I could hardly write fast enough to keep up with these ideas. "And the berries."

"Let's plant a bank of deciduous hollies around the pasture. It'll take a couple of years to get enough fruit, but then you'll have plenty." He smiled at me. "Until then, I'll convince my ma to give you some from her bushes."

"Oh yeah, that's just great. 'Mom, the new American woman who is my boss wants to know if I can have some of your plants?' That'll make a great first impression." I laughed.

"Well, you've got a few months to warm her to you, haven't you?" Gray said with a wink.

"I suppose so," I said.

By the time Gray left just before dusk, the two of us had planned a full-on subscription series, and I had even felt bold enough to tell him the name for my business: The Statice Symbol.

His chuckle at the pun had warmed my heart, and as I made a bowl of soup from the can I found in the cupboard, I let myself feel right at home.

Slaying at Stanway: Chapter Two

When I woke the next morning, I knew two things: I needed something besides soup for breakfast, and I needed to get warm. Despite the fact that I had a radiator in my bedroom, I hadn't been able to figure out how to get it to work before I'd gone to bed. So I'd slept in a full sweatsuit, two pairs of socks, and a hat. And when I discovered that I also didn't have hot water for a shower, I decided it was time to find coffee – or, if necessary, tea – and get some hot food in my stomach.

Plus, I knew the walk into town would be good to not only help me get warm but also get my mental juices flowing. I had a lot to do, and I was eager to get to doing it. But I also needed to have a plan, not just the great subscription plan Gray and I had dreamt up yesterday but a full-on business plan that would make the most of both my time and the money I'd gotten from the sale of my parents' house. Such thinking required not only warmth but protein.

By the time I'd walked the half-mile into town, I was equal parts warmer and hungrier, so when I saw a tea shop with a neon "Breakfast" sign in the window, I hadn't even slowed my pace as I walked in. Inside, I was met with a warm blast of delicious air and the site of the most charming shop I'd ever seen.

Each antique round table was surrounded by mismatched chairs, some ladder backs, some wingbacks, some actual stools. Nothing matched, but everything aligned from the mix of modern light fixtures hanging on the ceiling to the framed pieces of wallpaper or fabric – I couldn't tell which – that adorned the walls. And the woman behind the counter with her mohawk afro, cheek piercing, and long broomstick skirt looked like she fit right in.

When I walked up to the counter to place my order, the woman greeted me with a hearty "howdy," and I felt a piece of tension I hadn't known I was carrying in my shoulders melt at the sound of the woman's American accent.

"You're American, too," I said. "I just moved here yesterday."

"You must be Nigella Hunt," the woman said as she put out her hand to shake mine. "Jasmine Jenkins. American by birth, English by choice," she said with a smile. "You, my dear, look like a woman who could use something filling and hot. Traditional English breakfast? Cup of coffee?"

Jazz phrased those two sentences like questions, but I somehow knew they were strong suggestions. "Yes, please. As long as the breakfast has sausage or bacon."

"Yes, ma'am, but here when people say bacon, they don't mean that delightful fried food we know from home. They mean what those of us from the American South call *Canadian bacon*. That alright with you."

"As long as it's from a pig," I said, remembering my grandfather from North Carolina and the way he'd rip off a piece of tough Canadian bacon with his teeth and savor it while he chewed. I wouldn't make a habit of eating the stuff given that I also had my grandfather's tendency toward high cholesterol, but today, I was all about the joy of this new place.

"Take a seat," Jasmine said. "I'll bring it out."

"Oh, thanks," I said and made my way to a small wooden table flanked by two massive wingback chairs. I took the seat with the best view of the room and settled back to take in what would probably be my new favorite hangout spot.

Within a couple of minutes, Jasmine brought out a huge mug of coffee, a tiny silver pot full of what looked to be heavy cream, and a full shaker of sugar. "I took you for a sweet and creamy girl," she said as she set the items in front of me. "Did I get it right?"

"You did. Impressive," I said as I began to pour what was definitely heavy cream into my mug and followed it with the three spoons of sugar. "Thank you."

"Mind if I sit for a bit?" she said as she looked over at the empty counter. "I have a lull."

"Please," I said. "I had no idea I'd find another American so quickly."

"Well, if you hadn't found me, I would have hunted you down later today. We ex-pats have to stick together." Jazz lowered her voice conspiratorially, "after all, we're the ones who call soccer by its correct name."

I laughed. "I expect the rest of the world would disagree with you on that point, but I'm with you. So what brought you here?"

"Actually, most of my family is here. My brother took a job down in Gloucester a few years ago and convinced my parents to come too. They all live on a sort of compound like thing in the countryside. I visited a couple of times and decided I didn't want to be left out."

"So you live at the compound, too?" I asked with a raised eyebrow.

"Oh no, no no. I didn't want to be left out of life in the Cotswolds. Daily life with my family I'm completely fine missing out on." She grinned. "But actually, that's the other reason why I was going to track you down today."

"Not just so you could encourage me to hold on to the word *soccer*. What, are you tired of the metric system too?"

Jasmine laughed. "Well, yes, but no, really, I kind of need to hire you."

I stared at my new friend. "Hire me? For what? Do you want help here?" I couldn't figure out why it would be important for me, in particular, to work in the coffee shop, but I couldn't hazard a guess what else Jasmine might be talking about.

"No, but if you're looking for work, I could probably find a way to give you a few hours." She looked at me sincerely.

"Oh, goodness. No, that's kind of you. I'm all set. But what *did* you want to hire me for?"

"I know it's totally last minute, but my brother's florist just backed out on his wedding this weekend, and Gray tells me you are opening a flower farm."

"Will be opening a flower farm," I said. "I don't have any flowers yet, so I don't think I can help. I'm sorry. I wish I could."

"Oh, we have the flowers. They've all been ordered and will be in from London on Friday. What we don't have is someone to arrange them." Jasmine grinned at me. "You up for a job this weekend?"

I stared at her for a long minute and then threw my

hands in the air. "Why not? Might as well jump in with both feet. Tell me what we have going on."

For the next few minutes, Jasmine described the theme of the wedding – Spring Magic – the color scheme – pastels – and the location, some swanky manor house to the South. She said they'd need to do center pieces, boutonnieres, and bouquets and told me I'd have a gorgeous array of roses, orchids, and other pastel flowers to work with.

"Okay," I said as I began to wish I'd brought a pen and paper. "And when is everything being delivered?

"It'll be at Stanway House at Noon on Friday. If you're free, we can ride down together on Friday morning and stay through Sunday. I have a room with two queen beds if you don't mind sharing."

"A chance to be part of a top-tier wedding and stay a weekend in an English manor house – count me all in."

"Not just any top-tier wedding. The most extravagant wedding of the year, if the tabloids are to be believed. And not just any manor house. This is the house that inspired *Peter Pan.*"

Grab your copy…
vinci-books.com/cotswolds1

About the Author

ACF Bookens lives at the edge of Virginia's Blue Ridge Mountains with her young son and three playful cats. When she's not writing, she cross-stitches, plays too much Roblox with her kid, and does historical research on enslaved communities in the area.

www.ingramcontent.com/pod-product-compliance
Lightning Source LLC
Jackson TN
JSHW030152231125
94676JS00018B/982